MW00914317

Ellie

A Story Of Profound Loss And Abuse

by

Deborah Rose

PublishAmerica
Baltimore

© 2005 by Deborah Rose.
All rights reserved. No part of this book may be reproduced, stored in a retrieval system or transmitted in any form or by any means without the prior written permission of the publishers, except by a reviewer who may quote brief passages in a review to be printed in a newspaper, magazine or journal.

First printing

At the specific preference of the author, PublishAmerica allowed this work to remain exactly as the author intended, verbatim, without editorial input.

Cover design by Shirley Colon

www.deborahrose.net

ISBN: 1-4137-8920-X
PUBLISHED BY PUBLISHAMERICA, LLLP
www.publishamerica.com
Baltimore

Printed in the United States of America

For my Heavenly Father,
who sustains me, comforts me,
guides me to be my best,
and lifts me up on wings of eagles

Acknowledgments

I thank Mr. Robert Clancy, who did his best to help and protect me. I hope you get to read this and know that you made a difference.

My dear friend, Shirl. You've been with me through so much. I love you dearly, and now you are also my wonderful editor. Thank you so much.

Neil Boston, for giving me the greatest gift, and for persevering in doing so, and for the gift of your daughter Dianna as a beloved friend to Stephanie.

I thank my children, because you also helped me to reach beyond myself and grow tremendously. You've helped lessen the emptiness in my heart, and I love you.

I thank my son-in-law Joe, for loving Stephanie, for making me laugh, and for laughing at fart jokes and The Three Stooges. Enough said, dude.

Audrey Lambert, thank you, with all my heart, for standing by me daily in 2001 while I endured so much. I know that wasn't easy.

Tawni Machado, hey girlie, singing in the car will never be the same without you. Thank you for the laughs and silliness.

With gratitude to Kathy Laundrie, Linda Hafeman, and Sandy Caruso who did their best to help me in whatever way they could when I was in Milwaukee.

With deep appreciation to Max and Janet Showers and their daughters, who made me part of their family while I lived in Pennsylvania. I have fondest memories; thank you.

Al and Kathy Frazier, thank you for your patience, love and perseverance. You always have a place in my heart.

I am grateful for every friend who has touched my life. All of you have helped me grow in one way or another.

I am eternally grateful to my wonderful mother, my mommy. She loved me with perfect maternal love, and gave me a model to follow as a parent. The inner strength I have is due to the foundation she built during my first seven years.

Table of Contents

Chapter One
A Day in the Life

She sat at her desk, tensely waiting and praying the timing would be perfect today. Her books and her purse were stacked in front of her, ready for a quick escape. She impatiently listened to the teacher while she kept a nervous eye on the clock on the wall in front of her. *Please, God, let her dismiss us as soon as the bell rings.*

Sometimes the teacher would say a few things after the bell rang, and she panicked at the thought of it. Her mind raced with thoughts of the sequence that must take place. The teacher had to dismiss the class as soon as the bell rang. She must hurry to the bus stop. The bus had to be on time, not early so that she missed it and had to take a later bus, and not late. *Please, God, please, please, please let the bus be on time. Please let me get on the first bus.*

If there was any flaw in this sequence she would be late getting home and the suspicions and questions would begin. What had she been doing? Who was she with? Was she with a boy? The mental picture of what she knew would follow made her heart race and her hands sweat.

She sat there, as she did each day at this time, and prayed that everything would progress as it needed to. She looked around the classroom at the other students who were eager with anticipation of going home. For them, freedom and fun were a few moments away. She longed for that peace and abandonment which should have been part of her adolescent life.

Instead, she sat in her last class of the day, English, her favorite, and prayed and worried herself into a near frenzy. The bell rang; the teacher said goodbye; and so began her daily race to the bus stop. She ran across the busy street and anxiously looked, hoping to see a glimpse of a bus coming towards her. Within minutes, there it was. She breathed a sigh of relief. She had made it through another day. She looked at the other students on the bus who were laughing, joking, and talking about dates or shopping trips with friends. She knew she was going home to a different life.

She approached her house, not with eager anticipation, but with dread and anxiety. What mood would her aunt be in today? Would HE be there? As she opened the back door, a cold and empty feeling washed over her. Her aunt sat at the table, silent, looking sullenly out the window. "Hi," said Ellie. Her aunt made no reply. Ellie saw a basket overflowing with laundry on the table. She was expected to fold it before she could begin her homework.

When she finished folding the laundry, her aunt said spitefully, "There's ironing, too." Ellie found stacks of oxford shirts from her cousins. She cringed at the thought of the tedious work ahead. It was repetitive, boring work made stressful by the fact that the iron had been making sparks recently. She had told her aunt. Ellie could see that her aunt was hoping for the iron to start on fire, but she couldn't understand why. Ellie gingerly turned the iron on and began the long chore of ironing the collars, the sleeves, the fronts and the backs of endless cotton oxford shirts. Sparks shot out from time to time and then, as was inevitable, the fire began. Ellie screamed and ran from the room. Her aunt ran in and extinguished the fire, then chided Ellie for being a big baby.

Now it was dinnertime and Ellie sat quietly through another tense meal. At least she hadn't had to mash potatoes tonight because that always meant complaints from her cousins over any lumps they may find. Like everything else, Ellie didn't do it well enough.

When the meal was over the next ritual began. Everyone left the room while Ellie and her younger sister, Cara, cleared the table and began the long process of washing and drying the dishes. Ellie always washed and Cara dried. In spite of their mutual misery in this home, there was often hostility rather than closeness between them. Both were usually lost in their only escape-daydreams. It was not uncommon for them to flick each other with water or in some other quiet way annoy each other. Ellie remembered a time when they stuck together, but perhaps too many traumas and disappointments had eroded that. Now, even between Ellie and her only sister there was emptiness.

Ellie went upstairs to her bedroom to do homework. When she was through, the next ritual of her day began. Everything in Ellie's life was planned and dictated to her. She was required to take a bath every night and set her hair. She had been allowed to take a shower if she chose, but her aunt decided Ellie had "faked" showering so she must take a bath in order to be heard splashing in the water. Ellie took the tube of Prell Concentrate and washed her hair under the running water, wishing she could try a different shampoo. She hated the smell of Prell, but her aunt always bought exactly the same things and never tried anything new. Ellie vowed that if she ever broke free, she would never again use Prell, Zest, Palmolive dish liquid, or any of the other things her aunt used month after month, year after year. *She has no imagination*, Ellie thought. After her bath, she set her hair with the stiff, scratchy brush rollers that dug into her scalp as she tried to sleep at night.

While Ellie was in the bath her aunt would come up to her room and pick out Ellie's clothes for the next day. Clothing which her aunt chose and purchased. Ellie was often embarrassed by her clothes but could never tell her aunt that. She would sometimes roll her skirt at the waist to make it short. In the 60s, there was a standard of dress that everyone was expected to follow. There was no room for individuality, and Ellie never felt like she fit in. Once her aunt had bought her a pair of sandals. They were "old lady sandals" and nothing like what was popular among the girls at school. Ellie felt her skin stinging as she saw girls on the bus staring at her feet. Every day her aunt would ask her about wearing the sandals and Ellie tried to make excuses.

After she performed all the required rituals, Ellie went to bed at the set bedtime. As she did every night, Ellie prayed to God, *Please, help me.*

Thankfully on this night, HE hadn't been there. This was a good day. One of relative peace and calm. On this night she wouldn't pray to God to please, please let her die in her sleep. But there would be plenty of other nights when she would.

Chapter Two
She Always Brought Us Popsicles

It wasn't always this way. She had started out as the firstborn child of loving parents. When she was three, a baby brother was born and the family moved into a brand new home in a brand new subdivision. She was a feisty little girl who loved to play outdoors with her neighborhood friends. When she was four and a half, her sister was born.

What she remembered about her mother was her unconditional love. She read the children stories every night and sang to them in her beautiful voice. She had made a demo record with some friends right before she joined the Coast Guard, before she was married. She put jelly on scrambled eggs so Ellie would eat them. When she went on a diet, she ate canned shrimp and always gave a few to Ellie. She loved Ellie's father very much and Ellie felt a blissful security in her presence.

Ellie's father wasn't as warm as her mother, but she had memories of him playing baseball with her and her brother and of play wrestling on the living room floor. She remembered him taking her to buy Chicken Delight and ice cream in the summer.

In the summer, they often had family picnics with Ellie's mother's family. She had lots of cousins to play with. They spent less time with her father's side of the family. Her uncles frightened her, and her relatives on her father's side were not warm and affectionate like her mother's family.

The summer Ellie turned seven, the family planned their first family vacation. They rented a cabin on a lake and the neighbors waved to them as they drove off. The drive was long, and on the way they stopped at a store where Ellie's mom bought her an Indian doll. During the afternoon of the day they arrived, they went for a ride in a canoe. The lake was peaceful on that calm, sunny day. After they had been on the lake for a while, Ellie's mother started to complain of a headache. Her father rowed back to shore so

Ellie's mom could take some aspirin, and her father stayed in the water with the children. There was a slide in the water and while Ellie's dad held onto her brother and sister, she went down the slide into the water, over and over. When her mother joined them, Ellie said, "Mommy, watch me!" While her mother watched, Ellie went down the slide. She did this several times before Ellie said again, "Mommy, watch me," but this time there was no answer. She repeated it a few more times with no response. The feisty girl became angry and thought to herself, *I'll show her! I'll go down and she'll be sorry she missed me,* and down she went.

When Ellie got off the slide, she realized her mother hadn't ignored her. She turned to her parents and saw her mother slumped over in her father's arms as he frantically held on to her little sister with one hand. Her brother was screaming in the water beside him, and Ellie could only watch and wonder what was happening. A woman on shore called out to a man who was swimming, telling him to help her father. The man took her siblings while her father carried her mother to shore. He laid her down on the sand. This was Ellie's last memory of her mother alive-unconscious and foaming at the mouth as she lay in the sand. An ambulance came for her mother, and Ellie's father went along.

The children were left alone with the strangers who ran the resort. For a while, they stayed in the resort bar. Ellie sat on some steps alone, scared, and wanting her parents. The owners decided to put the children to bed in their cabin and then left them there alone. By now, it was dark outside. It was much darker than back at home, and Ellie and her brother began to cry. They became more and more frightened and their cries escalated to screams of "HELP! HELP! HELP!!!!!!!!" Nobody came. Her sister cried by herself in the crib in the other room. Eventually Ellie's brother fell asleep. She heard the sound of her father returning, but he didn't come in to check on her.

The next morning Ellie stood by helplessly and watched her father sit in a chair and cry. She didn't know why he was crying, and she didn't know what to do to help. Later that day, her Uncle Eddie came and drove back home with the family. Ellie was told her mother was in the hospital and had to stay a while longer. After the long drive home, they found the neighbors in front of Ellie's house, waiting for them. They talked briefly and Ellie's father told her to go inside. He took the children into Ellie's bedroom, and they all sat on the bed. "Mommy's dead," he blurted out and then broke into sobs.

Ellie immediately got up and went to her best friend Christine's house. She told her, as calm as can be, "My mommy's dead." Christine already knew, she said. Ellie asked, "Remember how she used to bring us Popsicles when we were on the swing set?" And that was it. Ellie went off to play, unfazed.

A few days later, they went to the church for her funeral. Ellie's dad picked out a dress for her. "This was Mommy's favorite dress on you," he said.

Ellie went up to the coffin with her cousin, who told Ellie that she shouldn't touch her mother or she would get germs. Ellie leaned over anyway and kissed her mother's face. Somehow, as she looked at her mother's stillness, Ellie didn't feel sadness or grief. The pain was somewhere hidden deep inside her, in a place her young mind and heart were unable to access. Her father cried during the service, and that's all she remembered. Ellie never cried for her mother's death. Not then, anyway.

Several weeks later, her father invited all of Ellie's aunts over to go through her mother's clothes. One aunt came by a day early, to get first dibs on a new dress that her mother had bought right before she died. The evening of the "vulture invasion" her father left. He piled all of her mother's clothes on the kitchen table. The aunts gleefully dug through everything. Ellie stood in the living room, watching them grab clothes and squeal with delight. She became angry. Didn't they know those were her mother's things?

Ellie saw a wallet on the table. It was her mother's; she had gotten it on a trip to Mexico. Ellie grabbed the wallet and ran to her room. She wanted to have something from her mom, but as she put it into her dresser an aunt came in and demanded it back. Ellie was never given anything from her mother. She was never given a hug or any other gesture of comfort, either. "They are kids. They don't understand what's happening," was the attitude everyone had. Ellie carried bitter memories of the night her relatives acted like vultures over her mother's things.

At first, neighbors helped with Ellie and her siblings while her dad worked. Then an aunt and her grandmother took turns. This seemed to be hard on everyone, and one day in the fall, her dad took the kids to see a man in a second floor apartment. He was the consul for a Central American country. Her dad explained that a lady was going to come to live with them as their housekeeper and she only spoke Spanish. Ellie thought that was an exciting concept and told Christine, who taught her to say *Si!* Ellie proudly used this word when they went to pick up Maria.

Ellie had only vague memories of that winter. In the spring, her dad married Maria, but didn't seem happy about it. Eventually, they told Ellie that a new baby was on the way. Over the course of time that Maria had been with them, Ellie had learned to speak Spanish quite well as Maria learned English.

One morning when Ellie got up, her dad said Maria was at the hospital and had given birth to a baby girl. Ellie's father seemed sad and tense. She didn't learn until many years later that his friends and co-workers were very upset with him for marrying Maria and having a baby so soon after her mother's death. The baby was born only a few days after the first anniversary of her mother's death. The next day, her dad was very upset because Maria had named the baby after Ellie's mother. He stayed in his room and didn't want to talk to anyone.

Ellie and her father both came home for lunch every day. When the baby was nine days old, Ellie was in the bathroom after lunch, brushing her teeth. She saw her father outside the bathroom door, staring at her. "I might be late coming home from work," he said. He told her he had a doctor's appointment. He kept looking at Ellie, like he was trying to take in the image of her, as if it were the last time.

There was a sadness about her father that she could sense, but not understand. Ellie felt the difference, but acted aloof and said, "Okay." He told her goodbye, and she just kept brushing her teeth. That was the last time she ever saw him alive.

She arrived home from school that afternoon to find Maria crying and her Uncle Ed on the phone. They told Ellie that her father was in the hospital. Shortly after, they said he was dead. Ellie played over and over in her mind their last conversation, and regretted that she hadn't said goodbye to him. She felt that might have changed things somehow.

A year had made a big difference to Ellie, who was now eight and very able to comprehend the concept of her father's death. This time she did cry, and she felt despair and fear. The next day, Ellie and her siblings were taken to the funeral home to see their father in his open casket. Ellie went up to him as she had with her mother, but this time she found herself shocked and frightened. HIS LIPS WERE BLUE.

She stayed at the other end of the room, afraid to be near him, afraid to look. His cold stillness, the lack of expression on his blue-tinged face, and seeing him in a coffin filled Ellie with terror. When her relatives saw how upset she was the children were taken home and put to bed, but when Ellie closed her eyes, all she could see was her father lying there with blue lips. She cried out and turned on the light, but she was still haunted by the image of his face. Crying hysterically, she didn't know how to flee from the image imbedded in her mind's eye. A neighbor happened to be there and took Ellie home with him. She stayed there a few days and was permitted to miss the funeral.

Life after this was hard for Ellie. Maria was left with a newborn and four children, including her own son from a previous marriage. She was frustrated and angry, and took it out on the children. Ellie became responsible for much of the care of the other children, and was beaten for any mistake she made. She had to watch her own brother and sister beaten as well and was helpless to stop it. Ellie began waking in the middle of the night and vomiting. Maria taught her to make Alka-seltzer and this became Ellie's nighttime routine: she awoke in the middle of the night, went by herself to the bathroom to vomit, and then to the kitchen to make herself Alka-Seltzer, and then back to bed, by herself.

At Christmas, Ellie made a nativity set for her room out of paper. This was the beginning of her interest in drawing. She was on her own a lot, lost in her own thoughts. To escape relatives gossiping about her parents or the stress of the household, Ellie escaped into her room. She often heard relatives talking badly about her parents and it made her burn with anger. Her relatives were angry because her father hadn't left a will and they were left trying to settle his estate and provide for Ellie and her siblings.

One night, Ellie had a dream about her father. In the dream, her father was there in her room, coming to get her. She woke in the middle of the crisp, snowy winter night and looked out her window. She looked up at the starry sky and thought if she just wished hard enough, prayed hard enough, her father would come down from heaven to get her. *Daddy, please come back.* But he didn't. She was alone, abandoned. The dream made her realize how very alone she was, and how much she missed her parents.

None of her relatives wanted to take her or her siblings. They had children of their own and didn't want the extra work, they said. So the children, for now, were left with Maria. Ellie missed being loved and nurtured. She felt vulnerable and scared. There was a despair within her that she couldn't describe and didn't know if she could hope for anything better.

An Uncle told another relative, in Ellie's presence, that her father had asked him to make sure the children had presents for Christmas if he wasn't around. Somehow, Ellie's father knew he was going to die. WHY? Why hadn't he made arrangements for them? Why did he just abandon them? Ellie could not understand that.

To make matters worse, she was ostracized at school and in the neighborhood because of her father's indiscretion with the dark-skinned woman. In spite of her devastating losses, children taunted her in the schoolyard and refused to play with her. Even her best friend Christine shunned her. She had no idea that things could get worse. And they would.

Chapter Three
Why Doesn't Anyone Want Us?

It was the last day of school. Ellie had finished third grade, and the teacher took the class to meet their new fourth grade teacher. While she was gathering her belongings, Ellie was surprised to see her Aunt Gloria.

"Why are you here at my school?" asked Ellie.

"Hurry up, we have to go home and get your things. You're going to live with your Aunt Sally and Uncle Gordon," she said sternly.

Ellie was confused. They drove to her home and Aunt Gloria went inside to demand Cara while Ellie and her brother, Craig, waited in the car. She heard Maria crying out and pleading with her not to take the children. As unhappy as her life with Maria had been, Ellie felt a loyalty to her and was angry at being taken away.

Ellie and Cara were taken to their Aunt Sally's house. They had only met their Aunt Sally and Uncle Gordon and their sons once before. For reasons Ellie didn't know at the time, Aunt Sally and her family didn't associate much with the rest of the family. They had a nice home, and Ellie and Cara were shown a bedroom that they would share. Uncle Gordon knelt down in front of Ellie and took her in his arms. He said he was happy to have her there, and Ellie felt a bit more at ease.

What happened next was devastating to Ellie. She was told that her younger brother, Craig, was going to live with Aunt Gloria and her family.

Craig had been born on Ellie's third birthday and she was a proud big sister. Craig was timid and shy, and Ellie would often play games with him and purposely let him win. Then she would praise him, and sometimes make little prizes for him. She loved Craig and felt a strong protectiveness of him, especially after the abuse he had endured with Maria. Ellie watched over Craig when he started kindergarten, and made a little book for him to help him learn the alphabet. To have Craig taken away was hard to bear.

For a month or two after this occurred, Aunt Gloria would bring Craig over to play with his sisters, but one day she informed the family that she would no longer bring Craig to visit. She said he got "too excited" after seeing his sisters. It would be two years before Ellie would see Craig again. She knew that Craig was sad and afraid at Aunt Gloria's and was picked on by her three sons. Once again, she was helpless to rescue her little brother.

For the first few months, Maria would call to talk to Ellie. She was upset and held on to hope that she would get the kids back. Sally became angry when Ellie talked to Maria in Spanish and told her their conversations had to be in English. Sally would stay in the kitchen while Ellie was on the phone, and if Ellie spoke in Spanish to help Maria understand something, Sally would sternly remind her to "Talk in English!" Once Ellie and Cara were allowed to spend an afternoon with Maria and see their baby half sister. She was now a walking toddler and Ellie had fun taking her in the wagon to visit her old friends in the neighborhood. That was the last time she would be allowed to visit or talk to Maria. She never saw her half sister again.

In the fall, Ellie and Cara were officially adopted by Gordon and Sally, and Craig was adopted by Gloria and Charlie. Ellie couldn't think of them as her real parents, and the girls were not even encouraged to call them "Mom and Dad." Ellie didn't know that they were receiving survivor benefits for the girls from their parents, who were both veterans of World War II. Ellie wanted to tell the judge that she didn't want to be adopted by them, but she was afraid to. Sally was so mean to them, and she rarely saw Uncle Gordon.

She and Cara adjusted to life at Aunt Sally's, but she had a hard time adjusting to the girls. Sally had three boys; two of them were teens, and a younger boy, Jerry, was about Cara's age. Sally seemed to be unhappy a lot of the time, and she became more and more unhappy with Ellie and Cara. She was cold towards them, and over time, added restrictions to their daily lives that made them almost prisoners. They were forbidden to join the family in the living room in the evenings to watch television. They were confined to their room and could not leave unless they were invited to. They could not get up in the morning until Sally came in and opened the curtains, and sometimes she would wait until late in the morning to do so. They could only eat what she set before them. They couldn't bathe unless she told them to. Sally didn't let Ellie bathe for weeks, and she got a thick yellow coating on her scalp.

During summer, the girls played outside and were also allowed to go swimming at a local pool, but when school began, Sally's mood became even worse. On weekends in the dead of winter, she made Ellie and Cara stay outside after breakfast until she let them back in for lunch, and then they were sent back out once again until dark. Ellie would walk in circles in the front yard in the snow and freezing cold that Wisconsin winter brought, trying to stay warm. There were few, if any, other children outside, so she and Cara would try to find something to do or they would just continually walk as the snow and ice crunched under their cold feet. Ellie hoped that one of the neighbors would see her and invite her into their home, but they never did. Sometimes Uncle Gordon would come home and see Ellie miserably circling the front yard, but he never asked her to come in the house. Ellie dreaded weekends.

Occasionally, Sally would do something nice. She bought some cloth and embroidery floss and taught Ellie how to embroider, and that is what Ellie would work on during the evenings alone in her room. Evenings were often ruined by Jerry, who would come in to taunt Ellie and Cara. He hit them because he knew he could get away with it. He would do things and tell lies to get them in trouble. Typical for a young, spoiled child, he took full advantage of his favored position. Ellie and Cara felt a burning resentment for Jerry and his mockery of their situation, but they were also afraid of him, knowing his power to cause them even more trouble.

One afternoon, Ellie came home to find five-year old Cara sitting in a corner of their bedroom. Ellie asked what she was doing, and she said Sally made her sit there. Cara turned, and Ellie saw the left side of her face covered with a large, red bruise. The sight of it was shocking to Ellie. She had never seen anything like it. The entire side of Cara's face was red and mottled.

"What happened to your face?"

"Sally hit me," Cara calmly answered. She explained to Ellie that she had eaten some snow, and Sally had slapped her and made her sit in the corner.

That night at dinner Gordon asked what happened to her face. Sally defiantly said that she had hit Cara for eating snow. Ellie hoped that Gordon would do something and Sally would get in trouble, but he said nothing. To see her little sister hurt and once again be powerless to stop it made Ellie burn with anger inside. She cried with sadness for her sister and buried the anger deep inside where it would not get her in trouble. Sally had often threatened to get the belt and give Ellie "the beating of your life." This made Ellie tremble with fear. She had experienced a belt with Maria. Ellie didn't like pain, and she knew that as hostile as Sally was with her, she had the potential to be brutal.

It was early spring. The girls had come in for dinner and Cara did something that made Sally angry. Some minor, insignificant thing that sent Sally into a frenzy. She demanded that Cara put on her coat and leave the house. "Start walking and never come back!" Sally shouted, as Ellie helplessly watched the small figure of her five-year old sister go out into the dusk and rain. Sally's boys tried to reason with her not to send Cara out, but she became more agitated and repeated the order for Cara to leave. Thankfully, Gordon was home this evening. He was rarely home. Ellie stood in the doorway of her bedroom, watching this happen in the kitchen. She started to cry with fear for her sister. Gordon told his oldest son to go out and get Cara. When Cara was brought back into the house, Sally went into a rage. She ran into the kitchen and grabbed a large butcher knife and lunged at Cara as Ellie and her cousins watched in horror. Gordon jumped in. He grabbed Sally and forced her into their bedroom. Ellie heard him slap Sally and heard her cry slightly as Gordon shut the door. He told Ellie to quickly grab some clothes and to take Cara to the car.

Frightened and crying, the girls got into the car and had no idea where they were going. They pleaded to never be brought back to that house. Between sobs, Ellie asked the question that had weighed heavily on her heart for the past year and a half.

"Why doesn't anyone want us?"

How does a child go from being beloved to being despised? Ellie had gone from unconditional love and encouragement to rejection and criticism. She felt no safety net around her. She and her siblings were vulnerable and unprotected. Now they were at the mercy of any adult who came into their lives, and there was no stopping any tragedy from befalling them. Ellie felt empty in her heart and there was no way to fill the gaping hole that her parents, especially her mother, left behind. Ellie had no idea where they would end up next, but she wanted to feel safe. She wanted to be loved, protected, and appreciated.

Chapter Four
Sandy

They drove up to a house they didn't know and met the stranger who would take them in for a while. Gladys was the mother of a friend of Gordon, a female friend, and one whom Gordon had been involved with for some time. Gladys ran a nursery school and was proud of the fact that one of her students was the daughter of a famous Milwaukee Braves baseball player.

Gladys ran a disciplined household, and Ellie was required to do many chores and always to ask, "Is there anything else you need help with?" before she could go out and play. Overall, though, their time with Gladys was calm and happy. Gladys' daughter, Sandy, would come over to visit with Ellie and Cara. She gave Ellie an old composition doll that was hers as a child. Ellie loved dolls and was thrilled with the gift, and with Sandy.

Ellie's trauma still manifested itself for a while. She became overly attached to a stuffed Dalmatian puppy, and would ask Gordon and others to give the toy a kiss and talk to it. If they weren't enthusiastic enough, she would cry out of pity for the toy dog. She carried the toy everywhere, and tended to it as if it were a real baby. She often cried over it and felt a deep sadness. Her own sense of abandonment and loss of love were projected onto this puppy, but would fade in time as she found security with Sandy.

Ellie was also accumulating an array of food experiences with each new home she lived in. From her mother, she remembered buttered noodles and shrimp; with Maria, she had experienced tortillas and Mexican cheeses; with Sally, it had been corned beef hash with scrambled eggs. With Gladys, it was Lazy Daisy cake and with Sandy, it would be Hungarian Goulash and brownies with powdered sugar on top. Her life was becoming a mosaic of family cultures.

When the school year was over, Ellie and Cara moved in with Sandy. They found a new two-bedroom apartment in which to live. Sandy, who didn't have children, threw herself zealously into motherhood. She decorated the girls' room in pink and attended to every last detail. An accomplished seamstress, she made the girls matching dresses and coats. She gave them a security they hadn't known since their mother's death.

Ellie's delight was the family rituals that they formed. On Friday nights, they watched the Flintstones. Sandy let them stay up as late as they wanted on Fridays, and they would try to stay awake long enough to watch *Thriller Theater*. Often Ellie's eyes burned with fatigue, but she lived for those Friday nights of TV dinners in front of the television.

Sandy worked for a dry cleaner near the girls' school and often they walked there after school to have dinner with Sandy, then all would walk home together. Ellie loved Woolworth's diner and their macaroni and cheese and tuna sandwiches. Another piece of the food mosaic in her life, this was a ritual she adored. Then one day something new came to the area-the very first McDonald's, right around the corner from the dry cleaners. So every Thursday, the girls walked to the dry cleaners and Sandy gave them money to go to McDonald's for hamburgers, fries and milkshakes. In those days, the biggest decision at McDonald's was what flavor shake to get. Ellie liked vanilla the best. These simple rituals meant so much to her, and gave her a deep happiness and sense of security.

Another thing that resulted from Ellie's newfound sense of security and love was that she blossomed in school. She was an A student and became one of the most popular girls in class. Recess was no longer a time of isolation, but a time of endless fun. Ellie felt free to be herself and the spunky, confident girl returned. At this point in her life, Ellie still had the ability to recover from the past traumas.

Two major things occurred during the Sandy years. The first happened in November of the year Ellie was in sixth grade. She came down with the measles and was very ill. Sandy worried about the high fever that hung on for days. While at home sick, there was nothing for Ellie to do during the day but to watch soap operas on television. It was Thursday, November 22. Ellie's soap opera was suddenly interrupted with a bulletin that President Kennedy had been shot. Annoyed, Ellie hoped that they would hurry up and get back to the soap opera. Ellie had become hooked on the soap operas because of her babysitter. Soon, though, came the sad news that President Kennedy was dead. Ellie remembered watching President Kennedy's inauguration on television with her third grade class. She thought he was handsome, and liked the fact that he had cute little children.

The next few days were a blur as Ellie, burning with fever, watched the endless coverage on television from her bed. It affected Ellie profoundly. She kept looking at the picture of John-John saluting his father's coffin, and Ellie's interest in drawing was rekindled. She spent hours and hours in class and at home working on her drawing of John-John. She worked and worked on the details, erasing and re-doing until she was satisfied. One day her teacher walked by and noticed the drawing. Ellie was scared thinking she would get in trouble, but her teacher looked surprised and said, "Did you draw that yourself?" He had the picture printed in the school paper and told Gordon that Ellie had talent that should be encouraged.

The sadness that remained following the Kennedy assassination would linger for some time, but something soon happened that took her mind elsewhere.

It was a winter evening when Sandy's younger brother came over to visit. "There's a new singing group from England and they have their hair cut like Moe from the Three Stooges." They all laughed at the thought. This was the time of Elvis and the Four Seasons, but it would soon change. Ellie, who swore she wouldn't like this new group, fell in love when she first listened to "I Wanna Hold Your Hand." Then they appeared on Ed Sullivan, and Ellie was now a Beatlemaniac. Because Ellie and Cara had teenage babysitters while Sandy worked, they had been exposed to rock music at a much younger age than most children were back then. Ellie wanted to be a singer like her mother and formed her own group at school. She nagged them to practice until they got fed up with her, and she lost a few friends as a result.

As she fell madly in love with The Beatles, she was growing into womanhood. Gordon took quite an interest in her changing body. He delighted in feeling her waist. At this point Ellie didn't sense anything wrong, and like most 11-year olds, she still wanted to focus on more childish things.

Sandy helped Ellie through these changes and was an always present security blanket. Ellie, Cara, and neighbor girls spent summer days roller-skating and playing with dolls. The upstairs neighbors had the new Chatty Cathy doll and all the girls had discovered Barbie. They would play on the front porch on summer evenings. Sandy would sit with them, smoking cigarettes and promising the girls that she would always be there. She promised that she would be at their weddings. She promised to always be in their lives. Ellie and Cara believed her, and thrived in the security of that promise.

In the spring, right before Ellie turned 12, Gordon decided to buy a house for them. Ellie didn't like the house much. It was very small and old. It had only one bedroom, which she and Cara shared, while Sandy had to sleep on the couch. It also meant Ellie had to switch schools yet again, and that she wouldn't graduate with the classmates she had drawn close to over the past two years. The new school was very different and although she made some friends, it wasn't the same. While her old school had planned a big graduation party this new school did nothing, and Ellie felt disappointed. For Ellie's 12th birthday, she got to wear stockings for the first time, and they went out to dinner at a Hawaiian restaurant called The Leilani. Ellie felt so grown up and loved the atmosphere in the restaurant. She was given an easel and drawing materials as her gifts.

Gordon had moved his oldest son from his first marriage into their apartment shortly before buying the house. His son had been in trouble and needed a place to stay. Sandy wasn't happy about having this young man with a bad attitude placed in her home. That and the stress of the little house caused tension, and Sandy seemed unhappy. Right after school let out for the summer, the girls were in their bedroom watching television and could hear Gordon and Sandy fighting. Gordon burst into the room, dragging Sandy by the arm, and yelling "Tell them!" Sandy just cried, and Gordon told the girls that Sandy wanted to leave. Cara, who was seven, started sobbing. Sandy was the only mother she remembered. Ellie was frightened and tried to comfort Cara. The next day, Sandy told the girls she wouldn't leave, and they felt reassured. That evening, however, she never came home from work.

Once again, their lives took a dramatic turn. Sadly, the security and love they had thrived on for two years was over for good. Sandy never came back, not even for her furniture or personal belongings.

Chapter Five
Doris

Cara and Ellie felt lost without Sandy. Ellie was angry and resentful. They had no idea what was going to happen, but soon would find out their next destination-Gordon's current mistress and secretary, Doris. They were to move in with her and her children. Gordon took the girls to his office to spend the day with Doris. Ellie liked her, but she wasn't Sandy. After the security and happiness they had with Sandy at the old apartment, Ellie resented the change.

A few days later they were taken to Doris' apartment to meet her five children. The first thing Ellie noticed was all the noise and activity, which she wasn't used to. The next thing she noticed was that Doris was a messy housekeeper, the opposite of Sandy. Ellie found these things annoying. Doris had two daughters. Noelle, the oldest, was very pretty and conceited. She was aloof and made the girls feel like intruders. The younger daughter, Roberta, was rude as well. Doris had three boys: eight years old, five years old, and the one-year old baby. The only thing that appealed to Ellie was the baby, because she loved babies. Ellie wasn't happy at all about having to move in here.

The next day, back at home, Gordon and Ellie were alone in the kitchen when Gordon asked her if she knew where babies came from. Ellie didn't, and Gordon proceeded to explain the facts of life to her. Ellie was horrified and very embarrassed to be hearing it from Gordon. He had been showing great interest already in her changing body and Ellie was uncomfortable with this conversation. It was the beginning for Gordon to use every opportunity to discuss sex with Ellie and a segue into ongoing abuse.

That week they moved from the little house into Doris' three-bedroom apartment. Doris' daughters had chosen to live with their father rather than with Ellie and Cara, so the girls got Noelle and Roberta's room. Gordon's

ELLIE

son, Ralph, had to share a room with Doris' two older boys. Doris and the baby shared a room. There were problems right away with Ralph and Doris. Ralph was very unhappy with the move and the living arrangements and clashed with Doris.

One day Ralph asked Ellie to go for a ride with him while he ran some errands. They ended up being gone until after dark. When they got home Ellie decided to be funny, so she climbed up the stairs on her belly and crawled through the open door saying, "I got decapitated in an accident." Instead of laughter, she was greeted by Doris and Gordon sitting in the living room and Gordon was furious. He bellowed at her "Where have you been?"

"We went for a ride. We were just riding around," she said.

"You're nothing but a tramp! Go to your room!" Gordon yelled in a rage.

Ellie ran to her room and shut the door. This was the first time Gordon had ever been really mad at her and it terrified her. He was a big, burly man and very intimidating when he wanted to be. He got his way by bullying people. He and Ralph had a big argument that night and Gordon kicked him out. It would be a few years before he would hear from Ralph again, but he refused to acknowledge his son.

Meanwhile, Ellie's fascination with the Beatles continued to grow. She was about to begin junior high, a new school where she wouldn't know anyone. Ellie practiced hard to learn to speak with a British accent and when she went to school, she spoke with that accent to her classmates. Before she knew it, Ellie had told people that she was from England and knew the Beatles. This brought her lots of attention and even the ninth graders wanted to be friends with her. In the cafeteria one day, an older boy heard that she was from England and was excited to talk to her. Ellie was uncomfortable with the lie she was living, but she was feeling angry and rebellious. The positive attention felt good after the upheavals of the past summer.

One day, Ellie was called to the guidance counselor's office. Word had gotten around about her ruse and the counselor told Ellie she needed to be honest with everyone. That was very humiliating and for a while after that, Ellie took a lot of ribbing. There was a young home economics teacher who made a mockery of her repeatedly in front of other students, which made Ellie angry and embarrassed.

In spite of it, the boy still liked Ellie. He wanted Ellie to go on a date with him, but she wasn't sure if Gordon would let her. The boy called her at home and Gordon bombarded her with questions about him. The next time the boy called, Gordon took the phone away from her and yelled at the boy, telling

27

him never to call again. The boy refused to give up his interest in her and called again. Ellie pleaded with him never to call her. She had to get angry and be rude to him, but after she hung up Gordon was still furious with her. "You're nothing but a tramp! You're going to end up in the gutter." At this point Gordon's wrath was a new thing, and Ellie was a little bolder in replying to him.

"I've never even kissed a boy. How can you call me a tramp?" Ellie ran to her room. It was very insulting for Gordon to say that to her. This only added to the resentment she already felt at Sandy leaving and having to move in with Doris. She felt frustration and turmoil within herself, yet still felt a measure of security.

Ellie had become aware of peer pressure and the need to conform. She was concerned with her clothes and hairstyle now. She spent a lot of time in front of the mirror and looking at magazines. When Noelle would come to visit, she always had a new outfit and always looked good. Ellie would observe her and want to have the same things. She asked Doris for a jumper like the one Noelle had. Doris bought it for Ellie for Christmas, but it wasn't quite the same. Roberta was there and made a negative comment about it. "Why are you wearing something like *that*?" she asked snidely.

"She asked for it," Doris said.

"No, I didn't!" Ellie lied, her face burning with embarrassment at Roberta's disapproval.

It wasn't Doris' fault. She really tried to make Ellie happy. She knitted sweaters for her and did what she could, but because money was so tight she could never quite provide the exact thing that Ellie wanted. Doris was working full time in addition to raising a bunch of kids. She wasn't the housekeeper or cook that Sandy had been, but she was funny and easy going, and she liked to take the kids for drives on the weekends. Her contribution to Ellie's mosaic of food experiences was deep fried shrimp. Her life was simple, but she did the best she could with it and rarely complained. Her biggest mistake in life was getting involved with the likes of Gordon.

Things with Gordon continued to get worse. He would frequently embarrass Ellie by bringing up things of a sexual nature. These things weren't discussed openly in the 60s, so it was extremely unpleasant for Ellie. Gordon began overstepping proper bounds. He would come into Ellie's bedroom and ask if her bras still fit her. Ellie resented this intrusion into her privacy and out of embarrassment would either sheepishly say, "I don't know" or not answer at all.

Gordon would then sit beside her and say, "If you're not going to tell me, I'll have to check myself" and would unbutton her blouse and feel her breasts, which made Ellie cringe. She was angry that he would touch her like that and knew that it was something that Doris could have handled, but she was afraid to say anything to him.

Gordon would sometimes ask Ellie to go for a drive with him alone at night, and he would always bring up the subject of sex. " Do you have any questions?" he would ask, and usually Ellie would say "no."

One time, though, she did have a question about something she heard at school. "What's French kissing?" she asked. Gordon insisted on showing her, and she jumped back when she felt his tongue push against her mouth.

Around this time, Gordon started tucking Ellie and Cara into bed every night and kissing them goodnight, but it wasn't a little peck on the cheek. It was a long, passionate kiss that made Ellie shrink back and detest this nighttime routine. Sometimes she would try to go to bed quickly without saying goodnight in order to avoid a visit from Gordon. He would get angry and expected her to come into the living room to say goodnight as his cue to come to her room. As he bent over her, she dreaded the feel of his lips on hers or the way he would move his lips around as he kissed her. It always lasted at least 30 seconds and sometimes his hands ended up in places where they shouldn't have been. It was revolting, and Ellie tightened up so much that she didn't know how he could enjoy it.

One weekend Gordon took Ellie alone on a trip out of town to a construction job he had. On the way, he brought up the subject of sex again. "The hillbillies have a funny custom. The boys have sex with their mothers, and the girls have sex with their fathers," he said.

"That's awful!" exclaimed Ellie. She knew this wasn't just an idle comment from him.

They spent the night in a motel and Gordon told Ellie "It's okay if daughters undress in front of their fathers." Ellie was shy and modest, and didn't want to inspire any more attention from him.

The next morning Ellie woke up to discover Gordon in bed beside her. Her pajama top was unbuttoned. Gordon said it had come unbuttoned during the night and he was buttoning it for her. He started kissing her and caressing her. When Ellie pulled away, he became angry and tried to make her feel bad. Ellie felt sick inside. It made her skin crawl to have him touch her, and now she had a dread of what his intentions were with her. She was apprehensive whenever he would want her to go anywhere with him.

After they returned home, Gordon became increasingly negative with her. He limited what she was allowed to do. Time alone with girlfriends was forbidden now because he said, "You can't be trusted." He also became more and more obsessed with everything she did.

When school let out the following spring, Gordon announced they were moving to another apartment. Ellie wasn't happy because it meant switching schools again. The neighborhood they moved to wasn't as nice. Roberta came to spend the summer with them. She and Ellie babysat for the other kids while Doris worked.

An incident happened that would increase the tension between her and Gordon. Next door lived a cute teenage boy, about 17. Roberta and Ellie had talked to him a few times and Ellie had lent him one of her Beatles albums. One evening Gordon came home furious and told Ellie to go to her room so he could talk to her.

"Did you give that boy your record?" he demanded to know.

Ellie trembled with fear at how angry he was. " I just let him borrow it" she said timidly.

Gordon slapped her, and after calling her a tramp and telling her she was not allowed to talk to boys, he demanded that she go next door immediately and get the album back. Ellie was extremely embarrassed to do so and was terrified at what else Gordon might do. She hoped the boy would be home so she could get it from him and she sheepishly asked for it back.

When she got back to her room, Gordon was waiting for her and was in the process of taking off his belt. He grabbed Ellie by the arm and swung the belt hard until she cried out. He made her go out to the living room and told her she wasn't allowed to go into her room by herself. The family looked at her, some with contempt, others with compassion. She found out later that Gordon had been pumping Roberta for information about what Ellie did during the day while he and Doris were gone. Ellie was humiliated, angry, and afraid. She knew she hadn't done anything deserving of Gordon's suspicion, nor to be called a tramp.

Ellie loved spending time alone in her bedroom to get away from the chaos of all the other kids, and to listen to music and daydream, and now Gordon took that away from her, too. Things were tense after that. Ellie couldn't vent her anger to Gordon and became withdrawn.

It was at this point that he really began to break her spirit. She didn't dare be spunky or bold. The spirited child who Ellie had started out life as was quickly slipping away.

She confided some to Doris, who would intervene as she could. She was kind to Ellie, but her loyalty was to Gordon. She was a single mother and had her own issues that involved a great neediness for this man, in spite of his nature.

Through one of her teen magazines, Ellie had gotten some pen pals and would correspond with them about their mutual love of music. It was a pleasant escape for her but when Gordon became aware of it, he demanded to read every letter from the girls, and every letter Ellie wrote to them, before she could mail it. Ellie was enjoying life less and less, but incredibly, it was about to get much worse.

In late fall, Ellie noticed that Doris was leaving newspapers open to ads for maternity clothes and was soon wearing baggy blouses. When Ellie said something, Doris would smile but not say anything. "I think Doris is pregnant," Ellie told Gordon one day, hoping to divert his attention from her, not realizing he may be responsible for the pregnancy. A few days later, Gordon said Doris told him that she was gaining some weight due to a medical problem. As the holidays approached, Gordon informed the girls that they would be moving back in with Sally!

"No, please, she hates us!" pleaded Ellie.

Gordon told the girls it was getting too hard for Doris to care for them, and that Sally had improved and wouldn't treat them as she had before. They were angry and very nervous about this move. Their memories hadn't faded with regard to Sally's mistreatment of them. Ellie was filled with a sense of foreboding.

They left Doris and would not see her again for a few years, but she would still play a pivotal role in their lives.

Chapter Six
Why Did You Take Us If You Don't Want Us?

This was the last place they wanted to be. Ellie was almost 14 and Cara was nine. It was Christmastime so Sally was in a decent mood, and perhaps to pacify her further, Gordon had bought her a Poodle puppy. It wasn't like Gordon to be thoughtful with Sally. Ellie thought this might have been a gesture to soothe Sally over the girls having moved back in. They were now living in Grandma's house. Sally and Gordon had moved in there while she was living with Doris. He had built an addition of two bedrooms and a bathroom on the second floor. Ellie and Cara got Jerry's bedroom, and Jerry moved in with his older brother. Grandma had her room downstairs, as did Sally and Gordon. Grandma had been her father's mother. Her mother's mother had died when Ellie was five.

Gordon swore that Sally had changed. He said his boys would tell Sally about things she had done to the girls and she would say they were lying. Maybe it was a temporary insanity, Ellie hoped. For a few months, things did go smoothly. Ellie was careful not to upset Sally, but Cara wasn't always obedient and Ellie would plead with her to do as she was told. Cara likely didn't remember what Sally could become.

Jerry was easier to get along with, and they would often play board games together. He still had an arrogance about him, and he always had to win. He did not have the restrictions on him that the girls had. Gordon's middle son, Laurie, was in high school and didn't interact much with the girls. The oldest boy was serving in Vietnam. Ellie started to correspond with him and they had fun teasing each other.

Ellie still had her pen pals, but Gordon stopped insisting that he read her mail. She had kept in touch with a girl from seventh grade named Debbie. One day she got a letter from Debbie saying her father had died. Some time after that she got another letter saying that she and her mom were moving to

California to be with her brother, who had just gotten a starring role on *The Mod Squad*. Ellie was sad that she was moving, and she never heard from Debbie after that.

One day, Sally answered the phone and said it was for Ellie. It was her cousin Patty. Ellie was very nervous because she knew Gordon would be angry that someone from her mother's family had called. After Ellie, Cara, and Craig were taken from Maria, they were kept away from their mother's relatives. Ellie's Uncle Ed had tried to keep track of them. He had found them at Sandy's and reported to social services that they were living with a non-relative. This made Gordon furious. Sandy had to get a foster license and Uncle Ed had demanded to talk to Gordon about visiting the children. Gordon had taken Ellie and Cara over to their grandmother's house, and Craig had been there with Aunt Gloria. This was the first time the girls had seen their brother in over two years. They sat on Grandma's front porch while the adults talked inside, and they could hear them yelling. The kids talked about running away together. After a while, Gordon came out and told Ellie to go in and tell Uncle Ed that she didn't want to see him. To keep Gordon happy, Ellie told them that she didn't want to visit her mother's relatives. It would be four more years before the girls would see their brother again. Due to that incident and knowing how Gordon hated her mother's family, Ellie was afraid of what Gordon's reaction would be to Patty calling. It was also sad for Ellie because Patty was the cousin she was closest to while her mother was alive. Of course, Gordon and Sally demanded to know what Patty had said. Patty wanted to meet her, but Ellie had to say no. Ellie wished that Uncle Ed somehow knew and would rescue the girls from this unhappy home.

Anything like this made Gordon and Sally even more suspicious of Ellie. They always believed that she planned things or was somehow involved. Because of this, Ellie was terrified of any unexpected contact from anyone and tended to withdraw from people as a result. Her mind always needed to be two steps ahead in any situation as she learned to anticipate how Gordon and Sally would react to things.

As had happened the first time they lived with her, Sally gradually made more restrictions on their behavior. This time they were allowed to be in the living room with the family in the evenings but were not allowed to change the channel on the television or touch it at all. They weren't allowed to open the refrigerator or cupboards to get food or drinks for themselves. They weren't allowed to answer the phone or the door. They weren't allowed to go to a friend's house or have anyone over. Sally chose all their clothing and set their daily schedule and routine.

It was an uncomfortable life, one in which Ellie always felt tension and anxiety about what might lie around the next corner. What mood Sally would be in on any given day was the main factor in the quality of Ellie's life. While Sally could be mean to Cara at times, her main target of animosity was Ellie. As a result, Ellie tried desperately to make her happy, to win her love, to be the perfect child. No matter how hard she tried, though, she couldn't break through to Sally's heart. In fact, the harder Ellie tried, the colder Sally became.

When school let out, Ellie learned what would be her summer routine for the next three years. She wasn't allowed to go anywhere so she sat in the back yard reading or writing letters to her pen pals all day, every day. She became a voracious reader as a result. She was allowed to go to the library to get books and often read several per week. She could see other teenagers walking past her house and how they were dressed and the fun they were having. She felt bitter at how unfair it was. She tried to hide out of embarrassment but would see the kids looking at her as if she were strange.

Sally had ups and downs in her mental state. During the summer Ellie was 14, Sally took a downward turn and became more hostile towards them. One day she was particularly angry and Gordon felt it necessary to take the girls with him for the day. Ellie was very upset, and in a bold move as they left, she replied to a hostile remark from Sally by shouting, "Why did you take us if you don't want us? You should have let us go with someone else. Why do you hate us?"

Those words, perhaps the reality of how her actions affected Ellie, seemed to spark a reaction in Sally. Ellie could see a look of shock on her face and she didn't reply. Gordon had a sly grin on his face as if he was enjoying the situation and then they left. The next day, when Ellie was coming downstairs, Sally said she wanted them to get along, and she gave Ellie a hug. She was sincere and seemed remorseful. Ellie was delighted, not knowing it wouldn't last.

In the fall, Ellie started ninth grade. She was feeling more isolated from her classmates as their lives became more socially oriented. At one point, her science class was going on a field trip and Gordon refused to let Ellie go because there would be boys there. The teacher asked Ellie about it several times in front of the class, rather than privately, and it was humiliating. He wanted to know why Ellie's father wouldn't let her go and she would only reply, "I don't know." The other students looked at her with confusion. She wanted to join after school clubs and hang out with friends like everyone else. Ellie's interests and potential in music and art were going unfulfilled.

In gym class, Ellie had another humiliation. All the girls were now shaving their legs, and Ellie wasn't allowed to. She was very embarrassed by her hairy legs. Other girls would make comments about shaving their legs and then give Ellie *a look*. Finally, she pleaded with Gordon and he got her Nair instead of a razor. He wanted to apply it on her, which she didn't like, but she was happy just to finally be like everyone else. Thankfully, Gordon let her use it by herself after that. When she would run out she would tell Sally, but got a cold reaction because Sally resented that Gordon had let Ellie do what she wanted.

Another requirement that Gordon put on Ellie was to tell him when she started her period, ostensibly so he was sure she wasn't pregnant. At that time there were no feminine hygiene commercials on television. It was a taboo subject, and one Ellie was painfully embarrassed to have mentioned in mixed company. As a result, she was hesitant to tell him, so he made a new rule: Ellie had to bring her used pads down to the kitchen trash. Her skin would burn with embarrassment, and she would pray that her older cousin, Laurie, wasn't in the kitchen. She would place it in the trash as discreetly as possible, but if Gordon was there, his eyes were always glued to her. Gordon didn't care at all about embarrassing her or hurting her in any way.

Things with her sister Cara also took a turn for the worse. It had begun when they lived with Sandy. Ellie was still spunky. When she was in sixth grade, she didn't want her little sister tagging along and would yell at her when Cara met her after school to walk home. Prior to that they had been close. If they had watched a scary movie, they would reach across their twin beds and hold hands as they fell asleep. Now, Sally would talk badly about Ellie to Cara, and Cara would sometimes even make up lies to get Ellie in trouble. Maybe Sally had let Cara think it would go easier on her if she spied on Ellie. The crazy thing was, Ellie had never been in serious trouble or done anything truly bad. She was obedient and a good student. But they used her lie about the Beatles when she was entering seventh grade as an excuse to believe she could never, for all time, be trusted again. They saw things that weren't there and searched to find anything to blame Ellie for.

Ellie survived by immersing herself in daydreams. They mainly involved musicians she had a crush on. The one thing Gordon and Sally couldn't control was her thoughts, and that is where she lived much of the time.

Things were about to get much worse for Ellie. She would need strength of both mind and heart.

Chapter Seven
Blue Cadillac

He drove a light blue Cadillac he had purchased brand new when Ellie was in sixth grade. It was quite a status symbol. Ellie had been proud of the car back then, but now it was something that inspired dread. If it was parked in front of the house when she got home from school, Ellie's heart sank because she knew he was there.

Drives in this car had been unpleasant ever since Ellie was 12 years old. Gordon always made her sit by him, and he would reach over and hold her hand, or put his arm around her, or his hand on her thigh. He often brought up sex. She hated going for drives alone with him and would slide over as far as she could to the passenger door. Sometimes he would say, "Why are you way over there?" and make her scoot over next to him.

Ellie was now 14. Gordon took her for a ride and said he had something to tell her. "The last summer you were at Doris', I had a tape recorder taping everything that went on during the day. I wanted to know what you were doing. One day on the tape, I could hear that someone was having sex, and I want to know if it was you."

"No! I would never do that," said Ellie.

Gordon proceeded to tell her that there was a test for virginity, and he wanted to do it to her. He wanted her to prove to him that it wasn't her. Ellie was frightened and didn't know what to do. She didn't want him touching her but knew he would never drop the subject if she didn't. Finally, hesitatingly, she agreed. He made her sit on his lap, and he pushed his fingers past her panties and inserted them into her. For several minutes he tried to stimulate her, but she tensed up. He laughed quietly to himself, enjoying the experience. Finally, he let her go, and she was relieved that it was over.

Shortly after this, Sally went into the hospital to have her gall bladder removed. One night, Gordon took Ellie alone with him to visit Sally. Ellie sat on the cold vinyl seat of the Cadillac, trying to inch away from him.

"There's something I want to tell you," he said suddenly. "I'm thinking of leaving Sally, and I want to know if you'll come live with me-as my wife."

Ellie's heart froze inside her. She kept thinking, *I'm only 14!* She was repulsed at the thought and horrified that he would even think to ask her. She had no idea how she would get out of this one. "I think I just want to be the kid," she finally said.

Gordon was furious. He rambled on about what being the "kid" would entail for her, and there were threats of beatings. Ellie's choice was either to be his mistress and endure sexual abuse or be the kid and risk mental, and possibly physical abuse. This was the start of the "no-win situation" she would forever be in with Gordon.

When they arrived home, Gordon was still angry and made disparaging remarks about Ellie and her rejection of him. The next day, he came home agitated and told Ellie and Cara that when Sally got home, she couldn't do anything around the house. "From now on you two do all the cleaning and the cooking," he said gruffly.

They were each assigned a long list of daily and weekly chores. Ellie had to cook the evening meal and fold and iron laundry during the week. On Saturday morning, Ellie had a full morning of cleaning, including the downstairs bathroom, as well as the living room, dining room, and kitchen. The bathroom was awful because Ellie wasn't allowed to wear rubber gloves and had to use Lysol concentrate that smelled of strong chemicals.

Sally was never satisfied with her work, although Ellie worked hard and never complained. Sally kept adding to the list as well. Ellie was required to move all the living room furniture and vacuum behind it every week. Then Sally decided the blinds weren't clean enough and Ellie had to wash those every week as well. She had to scrub the large kitchen floor on her hands and knees, and Sally complained every week that it wasn't clean enough. Ellie was very diligent in her work, trying to avoid criticism and to make Sally happy, but the harder she tried to be the perfect child, the harder Sally tried to find things to complain about. Ellie was never thanked for what she did.

Cara was responsible for the upstairs. Sally complained about her work at times, too, but generally she was easier on Cara. Still, there were times that Cara got in trouble. Whereas Ellie was timid and intimidated by Sally and Gordon, Cara was stronger and braver. Once, Sally got mad and slapped Cara. Ellie was very upset when she found out, but Cara calmly said, "I don't care. I could tell it hurt her arthritis, so I'm glad."

It was Ellie who became the main scapegoat in the household. Another one of Ellie's jobs was to clean Grandma's room, and wash and set her hair. She had always gotten along with her grandmother, but now her grandmother would sometimes betray that. One Saturday, Grandma and Sally were in the kitchen talking badly about Ellie, and loud enough for her to hear. Ellie didn't go anywhere or do anything, so there wasn't much that could be said about her, so they would pick at little things. On this day, they not only talked badly about Ellie, but about her parents as well. Ellie's father had been Grandma's son and Sally's brother. Ellie had to endure bad talk by relatives after her father's death, questioning his decision to buy a station wagon and other things they didn't like. It made Ellie furious to hear her parents talked about badly. As she sat on the couch, helpless to stop the conversation going on in the kitchen, seared by the cutting words and contempt in their voices, she began scratching her face. She kept digging her fingernails into her cheeks and scratching as hard as she could.

The anger and despair that she couldn't express verbally came rushing out through her fingers. She wanted them to see what they were doing to her, and she wanted them to feel bad. She wanted them to think about how her father would feel if he came back and saw how they were treating his children! She wished that it were possible for him to come back and confront them. She wondered what they would say if he did. She wanted to say to Sally "He was your own brother and we are his children. How can you treat us like this? Is this what he'd want you to do?"

A while later, Sally saw her face and said, "What happened to your face?"

"I scratched it," Ellie replied, without apology.

Sally didn't get angry. Ellie could see that Sally knew exactly why she did it, and once again, was confronted with the effects of her own misconduct. Sally bought Ellie some makeup to cover up the scratches for her ninth grade graduation, which was a week away. When Gordon asked about her face, she said that she scratched it because Sally and Grandma were talking badly about her. He didn't do anything about it.

Sally was nicer to her for a while and even shortened her dress for graduation so she could look like the other girls. Ellie loved it when things were good between her and Sally. She really did want them to be close. She longed for someone to take the place of her mother, to love her, appreciate and praise her accomplishments, to nurture her and to confide in. She never reached that point with Sally, but there were periods of time when they did start to get close. Ironically, it was Sally's awareness of Gordon's interest in

Ellie that put a wedge between them. Instead of protecting her, Sally felt resentment towards Ellie because of it and treated her worse.

Because Ellie was so restricted in what she could do, and tried so hard to be perfect, Sally had to really dig to find something bad about her. Often, what she chose to focus on bordered on the ridiculous. In the summertime, Ellie sat all day outside in the backyard, reading or writing letters. She sat in a chair and tried to stay in the shade as long as possible, but as afternoon wore on, less and less of her was in the shade. As a result, the tops of her feet were quite tan. Sally insisted to Cara and Grandma that Ellie must secretly be putting self-tanner on her feet! She harped on that for weeks.

Ellie felt always in a position of having to prove her innocence for every minor thing they may bring up. Life became a constant awareness of how any given situation could provoke suspicion in Sally or Gordon. She always had to be thinking about how she would defend herself. Just as she learned to read every nuance of Sally's facial expression and body language to determine her mood and therefore be aware of impending danger, Ellie learned to survey every single thing that happened to her. She couldn't just take in the experiences in her life, but had to always evaluate how Sally and Gordon would interpret everything. As adept as she became, they still managed to come up with things to question her about that surprised her.

Gordon had stopped taking her for drives alone, at least for now. However, the blue Cadillac would still play a terrorizing element in Ellie's life for several years to come.

Chapter Eight
No Sweet 16

Ellie spent most of her waking hours in her fantasy world, daydreaming about musicians and a life of freedom. She lived with disappointment over dreams unfulfilled. From the time she was 10 years old and plunking on the elementary school piano, Ellie had longed to be a musician. She had begged Gordon for piano lessons, but he refused. Now as a teen, her dreams went beyond piano to aspiring to the Broadway stage.

She was also fascinated with cheerleading and spent hours in front of her bedroom mirror trying to do the splits. Ellie knew that no matter what she dreamed or aspired to, it was unlikely to happen. She rarely thought of a life beyond this house. It was hard to imagine being grown, being free. She was surviving minute by minute as best she could, and any thought of the future was geared to worry about Sally's mood or if Gordon would be home.

Ellie received a letter from her pen pal one day in response to the confession she made about her home situation. Her friend, Kathy, told her about her faith in God, and sent Ellie a tiny little book of Bible verses. Ellie began reading it often and memorizing it. When she was eight and living with Maria, she was sent to Catechism classes. After that, when she lived with Sally the first time, she asked to go to church. Sally said they were atheists but allowed Ellie to walk to the Catholic church about a mile away. Neighbors who belonged to the church noticed the nine-year old walking by herself to mass and would offer her rides. Soon, Sally forbid her to go anymore. Ellie's spirituality was now rekindled and she tried to believe that God would see her through this. She attempted to have a joyful outlook and hid the little Bible books in her drawer. Because Sally snooped through all her belongings, she found it. One day Gordon confronted Ellie about it, and told her she could go to church if she liked. By this point in time, Ellie knew it would only be asking for trouble, even though she would have loved to go. Gordon and Sally would have used it as an excuse to accuse her of sneaking off with boys.

Ellie immersed herself more and more into reading, since it was the only pastime she was allowed. A turning point came when she was assigned *To Kill a Mockingbird* for school. She devoured the book in two days. She also found she loved the classics that Sally had told her she would hate, like *The Scarlet Letter, Les Miserables,* and *A Tale of Two Cities.* She read all the old 1940s mystery books that Sally had in her bookcase, too, but it was *To Kill a Mockingbird* that peaked Ellie's curiosity about slavery and race issues.

It was 1967, so racial equality was in the news often. Ellie read *Uncle Tom's Cabin*, which deeply affected her as well. When Gordon found her reading it, she told him that she felt bad about what slaves had gone through. This was a mistake, as Gordon was extremely prejudiced. He had demeaning slang names for every race but he especially hated blacks. When he saw Ellie was reading *Exodus*, he became even more agitated at Ellie's sympathy for other races. This only fueled his suspicions and fears about her.

Ellie's other outlet was television. She learned to be careful about expressing an interest in any show. If Sally knew Ellie really liked something, she would stop watching it so that Ellie couldn't see it.

Life by now was a tense dance which Ellie negotiated around Sally and Gordon's moods. She had no real life of her own. Life was something that happened around her.

Ellie came home the day of her 16th birthday to find a cake and a few presents. There wasn't a party or fanfare, but Sally did give her a brief hug and say, "You're 16 now !"

Ellie solemnly said, "It's not like it will do me any good."

In those days, being 16 was traditionally the age at which girls were allowed to start dating. Usually there was a big party with family and friends. Ellie had listened to classmates for months talking about their parties. She saw couples hand in hand in the hallways. She knew that wouldn't be her, but sometimes she would fantasize that it was. By 10th grade, Ellie had become very out of touch with her classmates. She longed to join school clubs and do what everyone else was doing. Because she didn't do those things, she lost most of the connections with friends she'd had in the past. She had a few friends who were considered outcasts who she would eat lunch with, but there were no shopping trips or hours spent on the phone.

As bad as things were, Ellie was approaching one of the most difficult years of her life, one she almost didn't survive.

Chapter Nine
No Win

It was fall. Ellie was 16 and starting 11th grade. Gordon took her for a drive one afternoon and parked in a deserted cemetery parking lot. He told her that she could start dating now. He said he would have to meet the boy and gave Ellie a list of requirements she would have to meet regarding her dates. He also told her that she could start wearing miniskirts. He asked if there was a particular boy she would like to date. "No. None of the boys even look at me because I'm so dumpy," she said.

Gordon seemed anxious for her to make these changes in her life but by now Ellie's radar was well-tuned, and she knew this wasn't a simple or pleasant change of circumstances for her. She knew she was being set up. Gordon had already been suspicious and questioned her about what she did during her lunch hour at school. He claimed he was having other students watch her, and that he would catch her if she had been in a car with a boy. Ellie was wise enough to know that if she did go on a date, Gordon would soon be accusing her of having sex, and maybe try his "virginity test" again. She knew any boy who dated her would be treated rudely and she would be embarrassed. When they got home, Gordon informed Sally of what he had told Ellie. Sally got a huffy look on her face and didn't say anything, but later she said she would hem Ellie's skirts. "You can wear them up to your ass if you want," she said angrily. Sally rarely ever cussed.

At school Ellie reconnected with a friend from Junior High who was now in her homeroom. Her name was Linda, and they would hang out at lunch. Ellie confided in her what was going on at home, and Linda was compassionate. Linda had a boyfriend, and they asked Ellie to go to a football game with them. Ellie had longed to go to her high school's football games and in a brave move, asked permission to go. She was told she could and made arrangements to go with Linda and her boyfriend. She had a great time cheering for her school. No negative consequences resulted at home. Gordon reassured her she could do what she wanted, so she began feeling braver.

Ellie needed a new winter coat. Shortly after she got one, Sally and Gordon started saying that they were checking it and finding buttons missing. They wanted to know how it happened. Ellie had no idea how the buttons fell off, but it became an increasingly stressful situation as Gordon started accusing her of fooling around with boys at lunch, which he said caused the buttons to fall off. Ellie was now worried all the time about her buttons and suspected that Sally was cutting them off at night. Gordon and Sally often searched through Ellie's room and belongings, looking for anything that might indicate wrong conduct on her part. As a result, Ellie was always nervous, since they often read into innocent things. No matter how good she was, they would always find something to be suspicious about. They had a way of musing about things sometimes, without directly accusing her, but it was always clear by the tone of voice that they were implying something bad about her.

Something else happened during this time. Ellie suddenly broke out in hives one day. She had no known allergies and had never had hives before. Sally had to tell her what they were. The hives became severe over the next day, and finally, Gordon had to take her to the doctor for antihistamines. The doctor suspected it was from a large amount of tomato juice she drank a few days earlier. Sally calmly and nicely asked her, "Ellie, you're not taking drugs are you? Hives are usually from a drug allergy." There was something about the way she asked and the look on her face that made Ellie feel that Sally might have something to do with her hives. One thing was certain, it fed into Gordon and Sally's paranoia about her taking drugs.

Gordon seemed to be getting more agitated. He kept asking why she wasn't going on any dates. This only reinforced Ellie's fears about his motives. About this time, she learned that a boy she had known in junior high, Craig, had been diagnosed with a brain tumor and another boy from junior high had committed suicide. One day on the way home from school, she saw Craig on the bus. He was pale and had a scarf around his neck. Despair and emptiness filled his eyes. Craig had been the class clown and always full of laughter. She was struck by the unfairness of it all. "It should be me. If it were me, it would be okay," she thought. It would even be a *blessing*. It wasn't the first time she had thought of death as the only escape from her life.

A few weeks later she learned Craig had died and Linda wanted her to go to his funeral. She wanted to go, but was afraid. Things were more tense with Gordon and Sally, and she felt going was too big a risk. Gordon was also highly agitated because Ellie had been talking about an English teacher she really liked. He was a big favorite among the students-and he was black. That put Gordon over the edge.

One Sunday, Gordon came home in a bad mood. He told Ellie to go up to her room so he could talk to her. Ellie climbed the stairs with dread in her heart. It was never a good thing when he said he wanted to talk, and especially not if it meant they would be alone. Gordon told her that he had been paying a boy at school to spy on her. "He says you've been fooling around with a colored boy at school. I want to know if it's true." Ellie denied it, and Gordon made a comment about her proving her virginity.

"No, not that again," Ellie said sorrowfully.

Gordon became enraged, perhaps because he knew that she didn't want to be touched by him. Whatever his reason was, he was furious. He swung his hand and slapped her as hard as he could. The force of the blow knocked her over, and her glasses flew across the room. He hit her again and she cried out.

"Don't you ever talk to me like that!" he snarled. Ellie went into a haze as he ranted some more and swore to "get to the bottom of this." As he left her room, he told her to wipe her tears and come downstairs. Ellie retrieved her glasses, but found they were broken. She also discovered a big gouge in her check from his fingernail. When she went downstairs, he was lying on the couch. This was his usual perch, like the lion lording over his pride. He saw Ellie struggle to keep her glasses on, and told her to bring them over so he could fix them. Ellie walked over to him and knelt on the floor, but didn't look him in the eyes. He touched her cheek and said, "Did I do that?" There was a sense of delight in his voice. He was in control and his power was unchallenged. Ellie remained withdrawn and frightened.

That evening, Gordon told her to come with him for a drive. Her heart was beating fast and she filled with anxiety. She wanted to flee, but couldn't. They went into the dark and he drove out into the country. For a long time he said nothing, and Ellie was frantically trying to figure out where they were going. Finally, on a dark, deserted stretch of road, he stopped the car.

"I've had a boy named Johnny watching you, and he says you're fooling around with boys. I need to know if it's true."

Ellie started to cry. Gordon slid over next to her and said, "You're going to do this, and it's not so bad." He reached his hand over and started unbuttoning her pants. He told her to take them off, and reluctantly, she did. "The panties, too," he said. She cried harder, and embarrassed, took them off. Gordon pulled her leg over, and inserted his fingers inside her. She tensed up, but also thought to herself that it would be over soon. He would know that she was still a virgin, and he would feel bad and they would go home.

To her utter shock he said, "You're not a virgin!"

"Yes, I am!" she said, horrified.

"ARE YOU CALLING ME A LIAR?" he bellowed.

"I don't know" she said, panic stricken, not knowing what to say or do.

She asked him to take her to a doctor to be checked, but he got angry and said that he didn't need a doctor to tell him. He demanded to know who the boy was that she had been with.

"No one," she said, sobbing.

"You've had sex with someone, and I want to know who it is. You're going to tell me or I'm going to beat the shit out of you."

Ellie was terrified. She felt stunned and was hardly able to think. She didn't know what to do, so she made up a story about a boy.

"Did he give you drugs?" Gordon demanded. Ellie said yes. He wanted to know what the drugs were. Ellie knew absolutely nothing about drugs, so she told him she didn't know. He kept asking her questions about what shape it was. What color. Ellie found herself engulfed in a lie she didn't want to tell, but she didn't know the way out. Gordon then started calling her a slut and a whore, and said, "I'm going to get some of this, too." He pushed her down and started to rape her, but stopped. Her heart was pounding. She felt sick and filled with panic. Time stood still as she was trapped and helpless to escape.

Afterwards, he drove her home and on the way, angrily told her how things were going to change. Any infraction of his rules and he would take the belt to her. He would check her regularly to determine if she was having sex, which he said he could tell by examining her. He was also going to find this boy she allegedly had sex with. Gordon thoroughly intimidated her, and she felt there was nothing he couldn't do. He had complete control over her. Ellie sat close to the passenger door. She was so terrified that she shook violently and couldn't stop. She was almost in a catatonic haze, aware of every breath. Her only thought on the drive home was how she was going to get out of this. There was only one thing she knew with certainty-she could not live another day in this situation.

There had been times when Ellie prayed before she went to bed that God would let her die in her sleep. Now it had to happen. As they drove, she thought of her cousin's razor in the bathroom. That would be the easiest and fastest way. There was no way she could make it through another day like this. Knowing she had a solution made her feel a sense of calm.

By the time they got home it was almost bedtime. Ellie knew Cara would come upstairs at 10 pm, so she had to act fast. She took the razor blade out of her cousin's razor. She sat on the edge of her bed, the side nearest Cara's bed, and tried to get up the courage to do what she needed to do. She was scared and hesitated, but then she heard music that signaled the end of the television show the family was watching and knew Cara would be upstairs in minutes. She took a breath, and firmly ran the blade over her wrist. She felt a sudden gush of warmth running down her hand. She was shocked at how much blood there was, but happy that she had succeeded. The blood was pouring onto the floor in front of Cara's bed, though, and she didn't want her sister to be afraid or to tell on her. She got up to get a cloth from the bathroom and left a trail of large drops of blood on the way. She grabbed a washcloth and started cleaning up the floor, but as fast as she cleaned more blood fell onto the floor. She got another cloth and wet it with cold water, and placed it on her wrist while she cleaned up. She barely made it in time and Cara came upstairs as she was finishing. She got in bed, and prayed with all her heart that God would not let her awaken the next morning. Ellie became concerned, because after she removed the cold cloth, the bleeding seemed to have stopped. She wanted to feel a change in herself, a sense of her life fading, but she didn't. She fell asleep and woke in the middle of the night. Her wrist felt tight and stung a bit, but she was still alive. She hoped that it would just be a while longer. In the morning though, she awoke. She hadn't bled any more. She was deeply disappointed and didn't know what she would do now. She figured she would try again the next night and not put a cloth on this time.

The next morning, Ellie got up and got ready for school. She had a gaping wound in her wrist, and a trash can concealing blood-soaked cloths. Her bloodstained bathrobe was tucked in the back of her closet. In gym class that day, Ellie looked at the exposed tendons and muscle in her arm. She couldn't concentrate on classes. Life felt very surreal, and she didn't know what to do.

At lunch that day Gordon appeared to pick her up. But his demeanor was kindly, as sometimes happened after he had been especially abusive. Ellie wasn't too afraid, and she knew she had her plan to fall back on. He took her to lunch at a Chinese restaurant, and while they ate, he noticed the cloth wrapped around her wrist. He asked her what happened and she showed him. She hoped it would make him realize how badly he affected her. He got angry and asked her why she would do something like that. He was angry because he would have to take her to the doctor and explain it somehow. He was angry, but not furious in a way that made Ellie tremble. He knew he had gone too far.

They told the doctor she fell on a Coke bottle. Ellie could tell by the way the doctor looked at her that he didn't believe her, but he made no effort to find out why she did it. She got three stitches.

Gordon took Ellie to stay with a family that had once hired him. They were a foster family, and Ellie stayed upstairs with their foster daughters. She would only be there two days, though. On the first day, Ellie didn't go to school. Gordon came to the home during the afternoon and dressed her wound. She was home alone, and Gordon asked her to let him see her room. She took him upstairs, and Gordon had her lay on the bed. He lay down next to her, unbuttoned her blouse and started fondling and kissing her. She tensed up and cried softly. She felt so angry that he would do this again, and so hopeless at her inability to escape. He got angry and chided her for not "wanting it." As he did when she rejected his advances, he got angry and threatened physical abuse. She became more withdrawn and cried. Finally he let her get up and he left.

The next morning, Ellie got up and tried to go to school as Gordon had instructed her. He had given her directions to get there on the bus, but they were wrong, and Ellie was in an unfamiliar part of town. She finally got on a bus that took her part way and she prepared to walk the rest of the way. She was already late. When she got off the bus, there was the blue Cadillac parked near the bus stop. She looked at Gordon and started to cry. "I got lost."

He then told her to get into the car in his best "I'm here to rescue you" voice. At this point, Ellie was emotionally crushed and barely able to think straight.

He took Ellie for a drive instead of taking her to school. He told her he thought she was going crazy and needed help. She realized that was an escape, and agreed. "I want to go to the hospital. I need to be in the hospital for a while," she said, crying. He agreed and called their doctor to have her admitted. Now she would be safe, she thought.

She *thought.*

Chapter Ten
Nowhere to Turn

Gordon had a presence that could be daunting. Ellie had occasionally seen someone stand up to him and he always responded with contempt. He especially showed a lack of respect for women. Ellie was at a loss to explain the women in his life-Sally, Sandy, Doris; all three let themselves be victimized by him. They craved him, but all Ellie wanted to do was run and never see him again.

He was a burly man with a distinctive square shaped head that Ellie dreaded when she saw the silhouette of it approaching. He often sat at the kitchen table in the morning in his bathrobe, chain smoking as he always did, and reading the newspaper. He had a gap between his lower front teeth which he would suck air through when he was in an agitated state. It was a drawn out, deliberate action that was often accompanied by an icy stare in Ellie's direction. He had a way of making Ellie want to disappear. She developed the habit of sitting with her head hung low, hunched over, trying to be invisible. She could feel his penetrating stare and feel the tension from him as he was approaching an opportunity to torment her.

On this day, Gordon had kept his word. He had called the family doctor who admitted Ellie to the small hospital where Sally had her gall bladder removed. The first day Gordon had left her there she felt some relief. The next day she had a visit with a psychiatrist. She told him the safe story that she had told Gordon as well, that it was Sally's treatment of her that had caused her suicide attempt. Later that day, Gordon came to visit her. He brought her half a dozen nightgowns and negligees. They were inappropriate for a father to bring a daughter, Ellie thought. They looked like what a husband would bring his wife. Ellie felt uncomfortable, and soon, Gordon had launched into an interrogation about boys and drugs. He told Ellie that he had the doctor do a pregnancy test and it was negative. *Of course it was*, Ellie thought.

Gordon badgered her until she became withdrawn and exhausted. After he left, she sat on her bed and sobbed.

The next day, when she talked to the psychiatrist again, she told him everything about Gordon. She took a chance, a leap of faith, that he would help her. He seemed sympathetic, but when Gordon came to see her, he was angry. He said that the psychiatrist said Ellie was "a paranoid." Gordon, in his usual persuasive way, had convinced the psychiatrist that Ellie was either lying or imagining the whole thing. Ellie had finally been brave enough to reach out for help and it backfired on her. She had always been afraid to run away because she had no one to run to. She knew he would find her and make her life worse than it already was. Now she felt very hopeless.

During their conversation that night, Gordon mentioned Doris. Ellie said that she missed her and wished she could see her again. The next day when Gordon visited her, he said, "If I was able to find Doris, would you want to see her?" Ellie said she would. The next day there was Doris, who seemed like an oasis in the desert to Ellie. She told Ellie that Noelle had gotten married and all of her other family news. She was kind and gentle, something Ellie hadn't experienced in several years. There was a comfort in seeing her again and being in her presence.

After this visit, Gordon talked to Ellie about living with Doris again, and Ellie agreed. She was released from the hospital, and on the way home, Gordon said they had to pick up Doris, that she had gone to her mother's house "to pick something up."

When they arrived, Doris appeared on the front porch holding a little boy about two years old. Ellie got excited because she loved babies. "She claims that he's mine," Gordon said. At that moment she didn't care; she just wanted a closer look at the boy. They drove home and later, Doris and Ellie talked alone. Yes, the child was Gordon's. Yes, she'd been pregnant when Ellie and Cara moved out three years before. Gordon and Doris now rented a house in an outlying area of Milwaukee. The little boy had the same build and facial features as Gordon.

Before she left the hospital, Gordon promised that he would never question her again about what allegedly had happened with her and a boy. It would be forgotten. They would move on with a fresh start. This made Ellie very happy. She was more relaxed with Doris. Her laid-back lifestyle was a relief for Ellie after the rigidity of living with Sally. Ellie was enrolled in a high school a few blocks away.

It was only a matter of time before things would go bad again. Gordon seemed unable to control his obsession with Ellie. Gordon came into Ellie's bedroom one evening and shut the door behind him. He said something had "come up" and he needed Ellie to give him more answers about what happened. Thus began an almost nightly routine of Gordon coming into her room and interrogating her until she collapsed into a catatonic heap. He drilled her about what kind of drugs she had taken, which left Ellie flustered since she knew nothing about drugs. He also questioned her about the mythical boy whom she said she had sex with, where they had gone, what days they had gone, what exactly had happened. The questioning could go on for 30 minutes, even an hour, or more. It felt like an eternity to Ellie, and Gordon's intensity exhausted her. One night, in desperation, she admitted to Gordon that she had made the whole thing up because she didn't know what else to do. He didn't believe her and continued to angrily pressure her.

Almost nightly, he would ask her what shape the drug was, what color it was, what the apartment looked like that she was taken to, what streets they had driven down. He wanted names of people involved. He was convinced that the popular black English teacher was the drug dealer, and he wanted Ellie to give him proof of it. Sometimes he would make Ellie go for drives with him, and he would drive around endlessly, turning down different streets, going far from home. He would ask Ellie, "Does this street look familiar?" or he would pull in front of a home or apartment and ask if she recognized it. Sometimes he would park the car in an isolated spot and start to kiss and fondle Ellie until she cried. He was desperately trying to get her to prove something that had never happened. In his own paranoid mind, she was involved with black boys and taking drugs, and he was determined to find the people involved. If Ellie had done these things, she would have told him and ended it all. The fact that it never happened and Ellie had no details to tell him made the interrogations excruciating. And more than once he had said in a booming voice, with rage in his eyes, "ARE YOU CALLING ME A LIAR???" Of course, there was no way Ellie could say "yes" without suffering his wrath, but to say " no" and have no answer to his questions left her in a no-win situation with no way out.

At school, Ellie was a lost soul. She knew no one, and was in such distress with Gordon's interrogations that she was unable to concentrate on her classes. On the verge of her 17th birthday, she had lost the will to live. She tried talking to Doris, and Doris could see how terrified Ellie was of Gordon, but Doris couldn't stop what was happening. The evenings brought sheer dread.

After nearly a month living with Doris and no end in sight of Gordon's harassment, Ellie decided to take action. One afternoon, Doris went to the pharmacy to get medicine for her little boy. Ellie stood behind her, and casually surveyed the shelves. She saw a row of sleeping pills, and scanned the labels to decide which would be best. As Doris talked to the pharmacist, Ellie carefully took two boxes of pills and tucked them in her pocket.

That night, Ellie felt peace for the first time in weeks. It would finally be over. She would no longer feel dread when he walked through the door. She would no longer be living in fear. She would never again experience the terror that rocked every cell in her body. While Gordon and Doris were engrossed watching television in the living room, Ellie went into the kitchen and downed the pills. She even drank some wine along with it for extra measure. She said goodnight to the family, claiming she didn't feel well and was going to bed early. She took the suicide letter she had written at school and tucked it back in a drawer. She wanted Gordon to know that HE was the reason she was doing this, and why. She went to bed, and once again prayed to God that he would, in his mercy, please, *please* let her really die this time.

Gordon,

If you're reading this, it means I'm dead now. I want you to know why. I'm not doing this because of Sally. It's because of YOU. I can't take you asking me questions any more. I never did anything wrong. I never had sex with anybody, and I never took drugs.

Since I'll be dead when you read this, I have no reason to lie. I never did any of that stuff and only said I did because you said I wasn't a virgin. Well, I am! I would tell you now if I'd done it. I can't take it anymore when you keep asking me all those questions about things I didn't do.

I don't want to live anymore because you won't leave me alone. You promise to leave me alone, but you always break your promise. I don't want to be scared anymore. How would you like to be accused of things you didn't do? I've always been so good. I don't give you any trouble but you don't appreciate that. All you do is look for something bad in me. You don't care how unhappy you make me. A father should not touch a daughter the way you touch me. I hate the virginity test you did to me.

ELLIE

I want you to know that this is your fault. I'm dead now because of YOU and you have to live with that. I hope you never do this to anybody else, and especially not to Cara. I hope you learn that if you treat someone like you have me, that it will end badly.

All I want is to be left alone.

Ellie

Chapter Eleven
Escape to Oz

Ellie was sitting in a chair in a hallway. Someone she didn't know was trying to feed her, but she couldn't eat because her throat was very sore. The next thing she knew, a woman was telling her to take a bath, and she sat in a chair nearby as Ellie bathed. It would be hours before Ellie could think coherently enough to realize that she was still alive and she wasn't at home. She was in a hospital, in the psychiatric ward. The nurses were unfriendly, and some of the other patients scared her.

At some point, Gordon appeared and did his best to make Ellie ashamed. She hung her head and sat quietly, trying to disappear. Then a nurse approached and told Gordon he had a phone call. About 10 minutes later, Gordon came back in a rage. Doris had found Ellie's suicide note and read it to him. He felt no shame, no regret, no accountability. Instead, he was furious with Ellie for writing it, and for being so "ungrateful for everything I've done for you." He berated her for what she had put him through. He talked gruffly about how things were "going to change" when she got home, and he didn't mean in a good way. He was furious that he couldn't just take Ellie home with him.

That night, Ellie lay awake trying to figure out what she was going to do. Would they send her home with Gordon? How could she escape? One of her roommates kept her awake by telling Ellie she heard voices and knew someone was coming to hurt them. The next morning, Ellie asked a nurse what was going to happen, and the nurse said she would meet with a group of doctors who would decide her fate. Ellie spent hours mentally rehearsing what she could say to convince them to keep her there. She planned a dramatic scene of telling them she WOULD kill herself if they sent her home. She was puzzled that her attempts had failed when all she wanted was peace. She wanted to be left alone. There was no way she could handle being sent back to live with Gordon.

She was nervous and shaking when they called her into the room. There was a large table and about eight people sat around it. The head doctor asked Ellie why she was there. She told them of her suicide attempt and why she had done it. With tears now flowing, Ellie begged them not to send her home. "Please let me stay! I need to be here. He won't leave me alone!" Prepared for the worst, as that is what always happened to Ellie, she was stunned when the doctor calmly told her that they had every intention of keeping her. She thanked them repeatedly, and for the first time, she saw kindness and compassion in the faces of people she turned to for help.

A while later, a man came to see Ellie. He approached her in a gruff manner, which frightened Ellie. Her sense of security was beginning to crumble as the man harshly asked her why she was there. Ellie kept trying to tell him about her parents and the whole story that led up to what her life was like now, but the man kept stopping her and asking, "WHY are you here???"

Finally, she simply said, "I tried to kill myself."

He asked why. She said that is what she had been trying to explain to him. He was being crude, and using profanity that made Ellie uncomfortable. When Ellie started explaining what Gordon had been doing to her, his demeanor changed. He was used to dealing with rebellious teens, some of whom had been referred by the juvenile court system. It took a while for him to realize what a fragile soul Ellie was. He asked her about school and she said she loved school. After they talked a while, he reassured Ellie that he would take care of her, and she would be safe now. And best of all, he promised her that Gordon would not be allowed to visit her. Ellie felt a huge relief and was deeply grateful.

That afternoon, Ellie and a few other patients were put on a bus and driven to another building. Ellie was taken to the third floor. "adolescent girls" was printed on the locked door. The staff was friendly and gave Ellie a warm welcome. She was put in a room with another girl. It was more like a bedroom than a hospital room, and Ellie was happy that her roommate was nice to her. Ellie found it easy to adjust to a life without fear and uncertainty. One evening, she looked at herself in the mirror. She was painfully thin because she had lost her appetite for months prior to this due to so much fear and anxiety. Her hair was dark blond and shoulder length. For the first time, Ellie felt like she might be pretty. She could feel safe in knowing that now that she didn't have Gordon leering at her. She had purposely worn her most unattractive clothes around him to make herself unappealing.

After a few days, Doris came to visit her. This was the first time they had seen each other since before Ellie took the pills. Doris seemed very concerned and filled her in on what had happened. She and Gordon had gone to Ellie's room when they heard her vomiting. Ellie was incoherent, her speech slurred, Doris said. Doris had urged Gordon to take her to the hospital. Gordon had called the family doctor, who told him to take her to County Hospital as he thought she needed psychiatric help. Doris said she had become upset with Gordon because he wasted hours arguing with the doctors and hospital staff over the phone as Ellie's condition worsened. He refused to take Ellie to County Hospital. Finally, after several hours, Doris said, Ellie was paralyzed and her tongue swelled up. She was unresponsive and barely breathing. Doris insisted that Gordon get her to the hospital immediately.

Doris seemed genuinely upset with Gordon for how he had handled it. Doris also knew that Gordon had been going into Ellie's room on a nightly basis. She knew how terrified Ellie was of Gordon. She had read the suicide note. For the first time, she was willing to listen to Ellie. She listened as Ellie told her everything she had been through with Gordon. Doris hugged her and said she would help her. Ellie felt so good knowing she was finally being rescued from the nightmare she had been living.

A few days later Doris came back to visit. This time she was distant and cold in a way Ellie had never seen. She acted with the same arrogant air that Gordon had. She said she had asked Gordon about what Ellie had said. Gordon had told her that Ellie was "paranoid" and a drug addict. Gordon was a persuasive person and managed to convince Doris thoroughly with his lies. Doris claimed she could tell that Ellie's eyes had been dilated on her previous visit and wanted to know what drugs Ellie was taking. She said she was going to continue the questioning that Gordon could no longer do. Ellie's heart sank. Why couldn't she have a happy life? Why couldn't she just live in peace like other kids? Every time she felt safe or hopeful, it was shattered. Now, though, Ellie had a champion in Mr. C, her counselor, the man who had come to see her at the other hospital. Ellie told him what had happened. Mr. C called Gordon and told him that if Doris did anything to upset Ellie, her visits would be terminated as well.

Gordon was not one to be told what to do, nor was he someone who took "no" for an answer. He was used to controlling everyone in his kingdom and did not take this turn of events well at all. He made frequent threatening calls to Mr. C. He threatened to hire an attorney to get Ellie released. When Ellie learned this, she sobbed uncontrollably. At one point, Mr. C had the head psychiatrist visit with Ellie. They had to make a case to keep her there. With Gordon's threats, they said they were going to have his parental rights terminated. The psychiatrist asked Ellie very intimate, detailed questions about what Gordon had done to her. Ellie cried with embarrassment. She finally asked if she could write it out on paper instead of saying it, and they agreed. Shortly after this, when Gordon found out their intentions, he backed off, but it would only last a few months. Gordon wasn't patient, and he needed to get control back.

In the meantime, Ellie was discovering what it was like to be a real teenager. The floor below the girls was the boy's ward and they often got together for group activities. The other kids felt like they were imprisoned in this environment, but to Ellie it was glorious freedom. She could eat what she wanted, wear what she wanted, hang out with kids her age, and most importantly, she never had to worry that Gordon would walk through the door.

Chapter Twelve
Don't Shoot Yourself in the Foot

In all her reading, Ellie had learned to appreciate different cultures. She was drawn to very ethnic-sounding names, and especially loved Irish names. The bulletin board on her floor held a list of the patients on both the boys' and the girls' floor and their activity schedules. One name jumped out at her, Kevin Flannery. *What a beautiful name*, she thought.

A few days later, all the adolescent patients were taken to a recreation room. Ellie looked around, wondering which one of these boys was Kevin. She spotted a red headed boy standing by himself, looking kind of like James Dean. Someone called out to him, "Kevin!" It was HIM! They exchanged a few glances, but he was aloof. He was a "bad boy," but she loved his name and was attracted to him. She went on all the activities from then on, hoping to see him, but they didn't speak directly to each other.

There was one girl Ellie especially liked. Her name was Debbie. She was 16 and pregnant. Ellie always looked to other people as a pattern of how she would like to be. She had lost herself and wanted to become someone with her own personality and tastes. Sally and Gordon had controlled her so much that she didn't even have a favorite brand of soap. Everything she had ever had was chosen for her. Debbie and Ellie eventually ended up being roommates.

One evening as they were walking across the complex to the recreation room, Debbie gave Ellie a very insightful comment, "You're not crazy. You just need to be loved."

It was true, and it was reassuring to hear it. Although being in this hospital wasn't an ideal situation, for Ellie it was a chance to grow and learn what it was like to be a regular teenager. With Mr. C's help and with the lack of abuse, Ellie could spread her wings a bit.

Things went well for a while; that is, until Gordon once again started demanding visits. Ellie was learning more and more that she could never believe or trust him. This time Gordon demanded a meeting with the doctors. Ellie would have to attend and it sent chills through her. Being spared any contact with Gordon for several months made the thought of having to see him even more daunting. The day of the meeting, they were all escorted into a room. Doris and Gordon sat next to Ellie. As was his way, Gordon tried to monopolize the conversation. He talked nonstop, as if he were trying to talk everyone into submission. Ellie was nervous, but she could see in the eyes of the doctors that Gordon wasn't pulling anything over on them. He was out of his league now. Ellie was asked to sit outside while the adults talked. After a while, they all came out. Gordon had his faux sweet persona on display as he knelt in front of Ellie and caressed her hands, tenderly saying, "It's so good to see you, sweetheart."

Ellie just hung her head and looked at the floor and mumbled, "Yeah."

He said he hoped she would want to start seeing him. "Think about it, okay?" he asked sweetly.

"Okay," Ellie said softly.

Of course, Ellie never asked to see him, but he kept pushing and the holidays were approaching. Meantime, Debbie had been discharged and a new girl had been admitted. Her name was Bridget. She had long, dark hair and wore lots of make-up, which she painstakingly applied every morning. There was something mysterious about her that intrigued Ellie. She looked like a folk singer and was a hippie. One day, Sally came to visit Ellie with her oldest son. Sally was very kind to Ellie. Obviously remorseful and a bit afraid, she seemed eager to make Ellie happy. She brought an acoustic guitar that Gordon had let Ellie buy from a pawnshop prior to her leaving home. Ellie took the book of chords she had and spent hours and hours practicing until she could do the fingering and play some simple songs. Achieving one of her dreams, to play a musical instrument, was wondrous to her. Bridget also played an instrument, and they became friends.

There was an open veranda in the back of the ward. On one side of it was a large open hole in the floor that was caged in. Through that hole they could see down to the veranda on the boys' floor. They weren't allowed to visit with each other, but they could easily sneak when there wasn't staff around. Ellie started having short chats with Kevin and her infatuation with him grew. The teens had a high school on site that they attended, and before and after class they had time to hang out. Bridget and many of the kids had used drugs and were sexually active, so Ellie started to learn about things and become more streetwise.

One fateful event changed Ellie's outlook. Doris had come to visit her weekly and would still make accusations about Ellie. Frustrated and tired of it all, Ellie decided that if she was always being accused of things she didn't do, even though she tried to be a perfect child, she may as well *do those things* and have some fun. This thinking, combined with the influence of the other kids, spelled disaster for Ellie.

One evening the boys and girls took a bus downtown to do Christmas shopping. As she, Bridget and some boys walked along, they spotted a young guy selling drugs. Ellie wanted to be cool like the other kids. She really wanted to be a hippie, and to say she had done the same things the other kids were doing so she bought two football-shaped pills. She was told it was mescaline, a hallucinogen.

Ellie took the pill and waited for it to work. After they got home, she started feeling the effects. Bridget was her roommate now and was worried about them getting caught. She took Ellie's other pill and began stuffing it in a duffle bag when a staff member walked in. Ellie had been very loud and was clearly "on something." The staff member grabbed the bag from Bridget and got another staff member to put Ellie in the restraint room. This was like the "Quiet Room," a padded room without furniture where a patient was put if they were "acting out." It had a bed in it and Ellie was tied down with leather restraints. She was left alone in the room all night, despite her outcries. She was hallucinating and became very afraid. She just wanted someone to sit with her, and pleaded for someone to do so, but she spent the entire night awake and alone. She didn't fall asleep until morning, when Mr. C let her out. He was very unhappy. Ellie had become so rebellious that Mr. C had lost his bond with her.

He moved her out of Bridget's room and forbid them to associate. He also told her that now he would have to let Gordon visit. Ellie's reaction was to put her fist through a window, which led to six stitches in her hand.

After having several pregnant girls on the ward with her, Ellie decided what she really needed was a baby. She had always loved babies, and she wanted something to love. She also wanted to be like the other girls, which meant not being a virgin. One afternoon she approached a boy she was good friends with and told him she wanted to have sex. He was happy to oblige and Ellie's first sexual experience was on a landing of some hard metal stairs in an unused wing of the hospital.

Gordon picked Ellie up on Christmas day and took her to Sally's. Ellie enjoyed the fact that Sally seemed so remorseful and intimidated by her, but there was something about Sally that inspired empathy in Ellie. Sally was like a wounded bird. She admitted to Ellie that her own mother had not treated her well. She herself had felt unloved and unwanted. To make things worse, she had married a man who was indifferent and unfaithful, although Sally wouldn't admit to that part herself. When Sally was in a submissive state, it was hard not to have compassion for her. Because of her remorse, Ellie could easily forgive all the mistreatment of the past.

That evening, after over six months of being free of Gordon, Ellie sat on the couch and endured another interrogation by Gordon. He wanted to know if she had been with any boys at the hospital. Ellie was now braver and had the safety of the hospital to return to. She also was only four months away from her 18th birthday, which was finally a glimmer of hope for her. She told Gordon about the boy she had been with. He was furious and said he would be talking to Mr. C and suing the hospital for letting this happen.

Ellie went back to the hospital. A week later Mr. C took her aside and said she was being released. Ellie cried and pleaded with him. She tried to run but a staff member caught her and she was placed in the Quiet Room until Gordon arrived. She cried the entire time. At one point, Mr. C came in. "You know what he'll do to me!" she pleaded. He could see that Ellie was genuinely afraid, and she had good reason to be, but his hands were tied, he said. Unfortunately, Ellie's attempt to be like the other kids, something she had always dreamed of, was now the very thing that was causing what she feared the most. She had assumed that she would be in the hospital until she turned 18. That had been the plan. But she had gone too far, and now they had to let her go or risk legal trouble from Gordon. Mr. C was compassionate and clearly worried, but he tried to reassure her. He kept saying, "You'll be okay. You'll be 18 soon."

When Gordon arrived he was kind and reassuring, but Ellie knew that couldn't be trusted. She somberly walked with him. Ironically, as they were going out the door, they passed the boy Ellie had lost her virginity to. She gave him a look to let him know not to say anything to her. She continued down the stairs, down to the blue Cadillac that was waiting for her.

Chapter Thirteen
The Trick

January 1970. Here she was, once again, back at Sally's. Grandma had gone to a nursing home while Ellie was gone, so she got Grandma's old room downstairs. Gordon told her they would put everything in the past and start fresh, and for a few months, he kept his word.

Ellie had enough credits to graduate high school in January so she didn't have to go back to school. Gordon had bills from her hospital stay, so Ellie was allowed to get work, and through the school counselor, she got a job at Milwaukee Children's Hospital. She went through a two- week training to be a nurse's aide, and in the evenings, Sally would help her memorize medical terms.

Ellie was fascinated and enjoying what she learned. Her desire was to be a physical therapist, but she knew she wouldn't be able to go to college. Sally's oldest son was attending college downtown so he usually drove her to and from work, but sometimes it would be the blue Cadillac waiting for her. Ellie would feel disheartened when she saw it, but Gordon was restraining himself. He did still keep Ellie confined to home and required that she sign over her paychecks to him.

The time away had made changes in Sally's treatment of her. Ellie had much more freedom of choice. She was allowed to dye her hair and choose her own clothes. She also had gotten into music that her hippie friends liked and she spent a lot of time listening to the Beatles' "White" album in her room.

Over the next few months, Ellie noticed deterioration in Sally's mental state. This had happened in the past. Once, when Ellie was about 15, she awoke in the middle of the night to find Sally standing in her room. She was in a fitful state and said angrily, "I know you two are up here talking about me. I can hear you, so you're not fooling me." Then she ordered Cara to get up and go sit on the stairs. Cara had been sound asleep and as Sally threatened to beat her if she didn't get up immediately, Ellie was frantically whispering "Cara, wake up!" Her sister finally got up, and in a sleepy haze, went and sat on the stairs until morning.

Now, though, Sally seemed fragile. She seemed to want closeness with Ellie. They had become friends and enjoyed each other's company. One day after work, Sally came in and sat on Ellie's bed. She said, "I have to ask you something. Is there anything going on with you and Danny?" Danny was Sally's eldest son and gave Ellie rides to work.

Ellie said "No," and in fact, told Sally that she and Danny rarely even spoke during their drives. Sally then explained that "voices" were telling her that Ellie and Danny were having sex. Sally was very calm and seemed rational, but distressed. Ellie reassured her that nothing was going on. She felt a sense of protectiveness over Sally.

In an especially odd move, Sally asked Ellie to contact Doris to ask her to come over and talk. Sally had found out about Doris after the baby was born. Sally was in such distress, and she had been isolated in that house for years, so had no one to reach out to. She wanted Doris to help her. Doris agreed to come over and the three sat at the kitchen table. Maybe the voices in her head had told her to do it or maybe it was desperation for a friend. Shortly after that, Gordon started taking Sally to a psychiatrist. Ellie had seen Sally angry and even violent, but never weak or helpless.

Now a month before Ellie's 18th birthday, Gordon said he wanted to take her out to dinner to talk about things. He asked what her intentions were once she turned 18, and she said she didn't know. Gordon told her that if she stayed at home, she wouldn't be allowed to date or go anywhere. Basically, he made it clear that it would be foolish for her to stay if she wanted to have a life of her own. Then he told Ellie, "As far as I'm concerned, you're 18 as of now. You can leave any time; next week if you want."

Ellie was amazed. A moment she never could have dreamed about was now here. She was free to leave this home and this life. She decided to wait until she was closer to her birthday, but she started packing. However, Gordon started pressuring her about why she wasn't moving out. He started getting irritated with her again. Two weeks before her birthday, Ellie looked in the newspaper and began calling apartments for rent near the hospital. She felt empowered by the fact that she was packing her belongings and had the freedom to leave.

One week before her birthday, Ellie asked Danny to drive her to her new home. She had found a room for rent near the hospital and when Danny dropped her off, she gave him a few dollars for gas and said, "Don't tell Gordon where I am." She had agreed to take the room sight unseen, but when she got there, she discovered it was a rather unseemly place. She didn't feel very safe there. She walked to a small store around the corner and ran into a girl she knew from work. She told her the predicament she was in, and the girl urged her to come talk to the manager of the building she lived in. Ellie was able to rent a very nice one bedroom apartment in her friend's security building. She felt like now she really had a home of her own. She unpacked and did a little decorating. She had three days off work during this time so she was able to fully enjoy the sense of freedom.

The day she went back to work she enjoyed the two block walk to the hospital. It was a warm, sunny day and she felt optimistic. During morning report, the clerk told her that the Director of Nursing wanted to see her in her office. Ellie felt nervous, not knowing what this could be about. When she arrived, there sitting in a chair, was Gordon. Ellie's heart froze inside her. "Your father has been trying to find you. Why didn't you let him know where you are?" asked the Director.

Gordon started telling her that Ellie was a drug addict and a host of other lies. The Director of Nursing told Ellie she had no choice but to fire her. And technically, since she wasn't yet 18, Ellie was a runaway and still under Gordon's jurisdiction.

Ellie was in a daze as she got into the blue Cadillac and they drove off. Gordon asked where she was living. He said Danny had told him where he dropped Ellie off and Gordon had gone to find Ellie, but she had already left. He said he had no choice but to go to her work. When they got to her apartment, Gordon took her by the hand and led her into her bedroom. He closed the drapes and made Ellie undress. He looked her in the eyes and said, "You owe me this."

He raped her.

It became very clear to Ellie that this was what Gordon had planned all along. He wasn't being generous in letting her leave before her 18th birthday. He purposely pushed her into a situation where he could get her into trouble and then take control of her again.

He decided to take Ellie to stay for a while with his sister Dorothy, who lived up North. Ellie had spent time with her before and liked her. Unlike Gordon, she seemed like a decent person. On the long drive up there, Gordon started interrogating Ellie again. At one point, Gordon asked if she was afraid of him. She said, "Yes."

Gordon was very offended by that and became even more angry with Ellie. "After all I've done for you, for you to say you're afraid of me is an insult," he snapped.

Trapped once again by him, back in his grip and engulfed by the blue Cadillac, Ellie sank into deep despair.

Gordon dropped Ellie off and told Dorothy and her husband the same lies about Ellie being a drug addict. The next day, Ellie had peace alone with Dorothy.

The following day was her birthday and Gordon came up. He took her out to dinner and then to a movie, "Butch Cassidy and the Sundance Kid." Gordon sat next to Ellie and put his arm around her. She inched away to the other corner of her seat, digging herself into the next seat until it hurt. Then he put his hand on her thigh, and moved it up as far as he could. On the drive back to Dorothy's house, Gordon suddenly stopped the car on the side of a dark country road. He tried passionately kissing her and started to unbutton her top. He said, "What's the matter with you? Don't you want it?"

"It's my birthday!" Ellie whimpered. She should at least get a break from his advances on her special day. It was her 18th birthday and she was trapped in a car with a pedophile.

Gordon got angry and buttoned her blouse back up. In a huff, he started the car and drove her home. A few days later, he said he was taking her home. He had found her an apartment and there was a nursing home up the street where she could get a job. He said he would leave her alone now and let her live her own life. She had heard that before, but she was 18 now, and she tried to hope for the best.

Chapter Fourteen
89 Pounds

Ellie now had a studio apartment in a nice building, and a new job as a nurse's aide in a nursing home two blocks away. Life should have been good now, and while she did enjoy a measure of freedom, there was a pall hanging over her in the form of Gordon. She never knew when he would appear. He would come by and interrogate her, or rape her, and then he would promise he would leave her alone. He always broke his promise.

Sometimes he would take her to Doris' house. Cara had been living with Doris since shortly after Ellie slit her wrist. It was sad for Ellie to see how her sister avoided her. Cara was aloof with Ellie. Gordon had convinced her that Ellie was someone she shouldn't associate with. The desperate measures that Ellie took because of Gordon were used to put her in a bad light and make Gordon look like a saint. Ellie bought her sister records that she liked and tried to win her over.

Another change was that Gordon had told his middle son, Laurie, about Doris and both Laurie and his fiancée spent time there. Laurie didn't have a problem with the fact that Gordon had a mistress and child elsewhere. Sally's troubles had caused her to be ostracized like Ellie. Two victims of Gordon's abuse were turned into enemies.

One evening they were in a restaurant and Gordon was once again trying to get information from Ellie about boys she had been with. Ellie had become withdrawn before, but now she was learning to withdraw so much into herself that she could become motionless with a vacant stare at nothing, and this time in the restaurant she practiced mentally lifting out of her body. She could feel herself looking down at herself and Gordon. She was there, but she was not there. It unnerved Gordon, and he took her home. Gordon didn't want to lose control of Ellie, so he kept threatening to go to court to get custody of her until she was 21. What he really wanted was to have Ellie living with him as his mistress. He even talked about them having a baby together.

The severe stress left Ellie in a state of anxiety all the time. She had very little appetite, and one day when she got on a scale she discovered she weighed a mere 89 pounds. She had a hard time concentrating at work. She confided in one of her workmates who said she knew a girl who needed a roommate, and Ellie considered the opportunity. It was very hard for her at this point to trust that anything or anyone could keep her safe from Gordon. The girl also suggested that Ellie go to Legal Aid and talk to an attorney about Gordon's threat of getting custody until she was 21. In a brave move, Ellie called for an appointment and took the bus downtown after work. The attorney she saw was impatient with her as if she was wasting his time. But the attorney assured her that as long as she was supporting herself, there was nothing Gordon could do. She decided to call Mr. C. and told him Gordon had been raping her and wouldn't leave her alone. She said she thought she might be pregnant. "Is it from your father?" he asked.

Ellie said "yes."

He was concerned, and urged her to try to get away. He also asked her not to consider suicide, but to call him if she really needed help urgently.

Ellie boarded the bus to go home with a sense of relief and joy. He could no longer hold that threat over her. She decided she would stand up to him and forbid him to see her. She mentally made plans of what she wanted her life to be.

She arrived home ready to really start her life. She put the key in the lock of her front door and opened it. As she did she was stunned to see Gordon sitting on her couch, smoking and glaring at her. It caught her off guard. He said the manager had let him in, and he wanted to know why she was so late getting off work. She stood in the doorway and said boldly, "I went to Legal Aid and talked to a lawyer. He said you can't get custody of me until I'm 21."

"Oh really?" he said sarcastically. "What are your plans then?"

Ellie walked over to a basket of laundry and started folding it. She was confident and aloof with him for the first time ever. "I just want to be alone here to live my own life. I don't want you coming over any more."

Gordon's reaction shocked her. He got almost an insane looking smile on his face and laughed in a manner that really made Ellie think he was mentally ill.

"You're crazy!" she said.

That made him angry. He got up and pulled her over to the couch, and made her sit on his lap. He was snarling about how she owed him. "You don't have enough of *this* in you to pay me back for what I've done for you," he snapped. When he said "*this*" he punched her in the groin for emphasis. He started up again about boys and what she had done in the past. Ellie escaped into her catatonic state. She gazed off blankly and was unresponsive. Gordon told her he would be back the next night and that he wanted a full list of every boy she had been with. He wasn't going to let her get out of it. He became concerned by how withdrawn she was and got up to leave. He made her promise she wouldn't try suicide, and he tucked her in on the couch. It was obvious he was shaken by Ellie when she reacted like that.

After he left, Ellie was frantic. She had not been able to relax in months. She always felt that life was surreal around her. It was hard to concentrate or enjoy anything when she had constant anxiety about what Gordon would do next. She got a plastic bag and put it over her head and went to bed, once again hoping she would die quickly and be free of this torment. As she laid there she realized it wasn't working, but she also was formulating a plan. She would go to work the next morning and ask her co-worker to contact her friend to move in with her.

She got up early in the morning, and was nervous that Gordon would come over and catch her. She quickly packed some personal items in a purse, and walked to work briskly, praying that Gordon wouldn't drive by and see her with two purses. She tried to hide the second purse under her sweater.

When she arrived at work, she was assigned her patients for the day, and she asked her co-worker for the friend's number. She explained what had happened the night before, and that it was vital that she get out immediately. Ellie went to the pay phone and called the girl. She woke her up, and apologized, but after explaining what she was going through, the girl told her she would be there in an hour to get Ellie.

Ellie did a few things for her patients, but she couldn't concentrate. When the hour was up, she watched outside and saw the girl, Cindy, approaching. Ellie grabbed both purses, and both girls walked to the bus stop. She simply walked out of the nursing home without telling anyone she was leaving. Ellie was shaking with fear that Gordon would drive by and see her, but Cindy assured her that she wouldn't let him near her. When they arrived at Cindy's apartment, Cindy called her boyfriend and a few of their friends to help get Ellie's belongings from her apartment. While they waited, Ellie told Cindy the story of her life, and Cindy was moved with pity for Ellie. The friends arrived and Ellie gave them her key. She urged them to do it quickly, as Gordon could show up at any time. The boys told her not to worry, that they would take care of him if he did. They were gone for about an hour and brought back as many of Ellie possessions as they could fit into their car. Although she was nervous, her new friends made her feel that she had some hope of being protected.

Ellie decided to call her friend from the hospital who was now living back at home. She let Bridget know what she had been going through with Gordon. The next day, Bridget called back and said that Doris had called her home to ask if Ellie was staying there. Bridget had told Doris, "He raped her!" and Doris responded by telling Bridget that Ellie was in love with Gordon, and for Bridget to tell Ellie that Doris would "step aside" and not interfere if Ellie would come back to be with Gordon. Ellie was horrified and disgusted. *How could Doris think like that?* She had daughters of her own. How could she feel that this was an acceptable situation?

The next day, Sunday, Bridget called Ellie again, but this time, she was upset. Gordon had called her house and demanded that they return Ellie to him. He said he had reported her as a runaway, and that he was going to have the police come and search Bridget's home. He threatened their family and also told Bridget to tell Ellie that he had gone to court and " proved her a paranoid" and been granted her custody until she was 21, so she had to come home. Bridget's mother talked to Ellie for a few minutes and was very upset. She told Ellie never to call again and to keep them out of her problems. She was obviously very shaken up by Gordon. Ellie apologized to her, but she and Bridget were both clear that they didn't want any part of the situation.

Ellie did take pleasure in the level of frustration she knew Gordon had now. She imagined him showing up at her apartment and realizing she was gone. He probably still felt he could threaten and manipulate his way into getting her back. It gave her satisfaction to know that he had no idea where she was and was finally helpless to get her back. She decided to call her landlord and let him know she had moved out. He was surprised and asked her why. "There's a man who won't leave me alone," she said.

"Does your father know this?" he asked.

"Yes, he does," she said. She hoped he would tell Gordon.

Ellie was both sad and angry to lose Bridget as a friend, but even moreso, she was appalled by how much Gordon felt he could manipulate her. Ellie was sound of mind enough to know that there were no court sessions on the weekend, that Gordon couldn't "prove" anything without Ellie being there, and that it couldn't have happened that fast. It really brought home the depth of Gordon's lies and manipulation of her.

Still, Ellie struggled with anxiety attacks. *What if the police were looking for her? What if Gordon found out where she was?* She had Cindy cut her hair short and dye it light blonde. This made her feel a bit less frightened when she was out. Gordon was self-employed and spent a lot of time driving around the city. He could be anywhere at any time, so Ellie never felt safe. Still, she would go out with friends to parts of town where she thought he wouldn't be. At that time, the east side of Milwaukee was where the hippies lived, and that is where Ellie and her friends would go.

One evening, as she was walking with two friends, they came to a corner near the bus stop. Ellie looked over to her right and there, with a group of friends, was Kevin Flannery! Ellie's heart leapt inside her. The boy who had been so aloof looked thrilled to see her. He rushed up to her and on that street corner, he took her in his arms and gave her the first real kiss of her life. It was magnificent; it was something right out of a movie. He asked for her phone number and address. He also told her he had written her a letter, but she had never gotten it. Gordon took all her mail. They would see each other a few times, but Kevin had sunk back into drug use. His own background caused him to push Ellie away even though he seemed comforted by her interest in him. He told her she deserved better than him. All of the tough kids that Ellie met saw the wounded, sweet soul that she was. As a result, she was usually protected, rather than threatened by anyone.

Ellie had walked out of the nursing home and couldn't go back. She and Cindy ran out of money and Cindy's boyfriend gave them enough to rent a room in a boarding house on the east side. Ellie loved Cindy and was happy to have good friends, but she was also tired of looking over her shoulder all the time. She didn't want to live with constant anxiety about Gordon and the only way to get peace was to leave the area completely.

Cindy had a friend in Boston who she felt sure would take Ellie in. They heard about a rock festival in Georgia, so Ellie searched for someone who was going and who would take her to Boston. She used her last bit of money to pitch in for gas with someone she didn't know.

On her last night in Milwaukee, she and Cindy went to Cindy's boyfriend's house. Ellie went out for a short walk. It was May 1970. She sat on the curb and looked up at the stars. She was exhilarated to be getting free, really free, of Gordon, and yet she felt a sadness and regret in leaving. All she knew was *here*. She was sad to leave Cindy, who had been her salvation. She knew she was leaving her little sister with Gordon. She felt guilt and concern for her, but also knew she was powerless to help her. In those days, she didn't have the hope of DNA testing and rape kits to prove what Gordon had done to her. She had too many people disappoint her, and too many times Gordon managed to get back in a position to terrorize her. The only thing she could do now was take care of herself.

She would leave the next afternoon, and she would never again come back to this city. She was finally free, but the road wouldn't be easy.

Chapter Fifteen
Boston

Ellie had not been out of Wisconsin since she first moved there at age two. She had never really thought she would be able to travel, and the prospect of seeing other parts of the country was thrilling. Her first introduction to travel was unnerving because once they reached the southern states, her group was in real danger from rednecks who didn't like hippies. Her male friends with long hair were targets of animosity and they had to be careful while in this part of the country. It made Ellie very nervous; violence of any kind frightened her.

Ellie had been to a smaller rock festival in northern Wisconsin shortly before she left. The one in Georgia was slated to be much bigger. Ellie loved the atmosphere of camping outdoors and hearing music while gazing at a starry sky. The aroma of marijuana and incense wafted through the air and everyone was happy. The second night there, Ellie and her friends walked from their camp to the other side of the road where the stage was, to see BB King play his set. The forested area and the clear night sky made it enchanting.

It was a three-day festival, and on the last day, the group that Ellie had traveled with decided to return to Milwaukee rather than drive to Boston. Ellie was scared and upset. There was no way she was going back to Milwaukee. Although nervous, she trusted that someone there must be from Boston and would be willing to help her.

She made a sign saying "Boston" and held it up to the passing cars. A van stopped and the people inside said they were going to Boston and offered her a ride. With a big sigh of relief she climbed into the van. One of the boys was very attentive with her and within a few days they became romantically involved. The group had planned to take their time driving back to Boston. One of their goals was to stay for a while in North Carolina on Cape Hatteras. They rented a small cabin and for the first time in her life, Ellie saw an ocean. She loved the sight and smell of the white sand beach and the ocean.

A few days later they drove to West Virginia to stay with the family of the other boy in the group. On the drive there, her boyfriend suddenly started talking to the other girl in the group, saying how he missed her and then he said, "I love you." She said she loved him too, and moved over next to him. They started kissing and Ellie was confused and in shock. She couldn't understand why this was happening. She had been so sheltered and really didn't know much about interacting with peers. That night she was still distraught, and the others in the group offered to buy her a bus ticket and send her to Boston, since they planned to stay a while in West Virginia. Ellie wanted to get away and without thinking it through, she agreed to go.

She said goodbye and got on a Greyhound bus the next afternoon. She had the address of the girl Cindy knew, but she had not contacted her to verify that she was still there. It was late evening by the time the bus arrived in Boston, and a wave of panic came over Ellie as she realized it was night and she was in a strange place and had no idea where she was going. An older woman who had been on the bus saw her fear and was concerned for her. She hailed a cab and gave the driver money to take Ellie to Cambridge, where the girl lived.

As they arrived at the neighborhood, Ellie became very afraid. It was an old neighborhood with barely lit streets. The driver left her in front of an old brownstone, and Ellie rang the doorbell. At first no one answered; then a woman came to the door, but refused to let Ellie in. She said that Cindy's friend, Shelly, no longer lived there. Ellie started to cry and pleaded with the woman to let her to spend the night. She had nowhere to go and was terrified. The dark, dark street left her feeling very vulnerable and alone. Finally, the woman let her in and allowed her to sleep on the couch. The next morning, she woke Ellie up early and pointed her in the direction of Shelly's new home.

Ellie walked in the early morning, hoping hard that Shelly would be there. When she found the house, she rang the doorbell. She was taken back when a Hell's Angel opened the door and started yelling at her for waking him up so early. Ellie apologized profusely and was relieved when the man finally called Shelly and let Ellie go to her upstairs.

Ellie told Shelly she was Cindy's friend and explained why she left Milwaukee. Shelly was very welcoming and they became fast friends. Ellie got deeper into the hippie culture. She loved the freedom that she felt because all of her belongings fit into a backpack. It was a life of freedom-no schedules, no decorum. The smell of patchouli and incense filled the air. Long hair, patched jeans, long peasant skirts, cow bells, face painting, macrobiotic diet; it was a whole new world.

Sometimes they went to Central Square to hang out, and there was always the chance to buy drugs. Ellie tried different drugs but almost always had a bad experience. As a result, she never developed the love for drugs that many of her friends did.

For someone who loved to read, the culture and history of Boston were very exciting to her. She spent hours and hours just walking around. She loved the cobblestone streets and the historical places. She rode a subway for the very first time.

Ellie relished the safety she felt without Gordon in her life, even though she had other challenges now. Still, there was always a fear within her that he would find her. If she caught a glimpse of someone with similar coloring or profile, she would panic and hide.

One big problem Ellie had to overcome was that she had no money. She went to the welfare office and was able to get an emergency grant, but she told them she really wanted to work. Within a week, she had a job as a nurse's aid at Tufts-New England Medical Center's Pediatric Unit.

Shelly decided to move back home, which left Ellie without the security of her friend. She and some of her acquaintances looked for somewhere else to live. Ellie used her first paycheck to rent a room in a large brownstone in the Back Bay area. Her friends depended on her to feed them and pay the rent, but Ellie was frustrated that they would keep her up most of the night when she had to go to work early in the morning. Most of the kids Ellie hung around with were runaways. They were all very young and immature, and often, thoughtless. Ellie started to feel used, but she allowed it because she was so afraid of being alone.

After a month of training, she was switched to the evening shift. That made sleeping easier but presented a new problem. She got off work at 11:30 pm, which meant she didn't get off the subway until midnight or later. It was frightening riding the subway that late, but not nearly as scary as the walk home on very poorly lit streets. Ellie's heart pounded in her chest and she walked as fast as she could. Sometimes her friends would meet her at the subway station, but there were many nights she walked alone in the dark.

In the meantime, she wasn't making enough money to support herself and everyone else. She often had to walk several miles to work because she couldn't afford the subway, and she and her friends would vacate a room or apartment late at night because they were behind in rent. Ellie managed to find new landlords to rent rooms from, but they never stayed more than a week or two in any one place.

As the fall approached, some friends started talking about going to California. Ellie had always dreamed of going there and knew the coming winter in Boston would be tough. One crisp October morning she and six other people piled into a van and headed for California.

Ellie now had the opportunity to see the whole country. Somewhere in the Midwest, they had an alarming experience. They were pulled over and taken to the police station. The officer was concerned about them being runaways. Ellie was afraid that they would contact Gordon. She looked very young for her age, and there was always a danger of being stopped as a runaway. Thankfully, she had gotten an identification card from the hospital and was able to prove she was 18 so the officer left her alone, however one of the other girls was detained and sent back to her parents.

Ellie's favorite place was Colorado. They stayed in Boulder for a time and Ellie found it breathtakingly beautiful. She almost stayed there instead of going on, but she didn't know anyone. Finally, about two weeks after they left Boston, they arrived in Southern California. Ellie now got to see the Pacific Ocean and was able to experience a completely different culture. However, Berkeley was the place to be for hippies in those days, so Ellie and two other girls hitched a ride there after staying in Long Beach for a week.

Chapter Sixteen
California

Ellie lived in Berkeley for three months. It was the mecca for hippies, although its heyday had been several years before .The major protests and revolts were over now. The entire time that Ellie lived there she was homeless. Days were spent panhandling on Telegraph Avenue or in the UC Berkeley Student Union. The homeless runaways took refuge in the Student Union during the cold winter days. There was an agency that set kids up with people who opened their homes as a place to spend the night. Ellie and her two friends from Boston, Robin and Muffin, spent the night at various places, usually sleeping on the floor. They were guaranteed one meal a day at a church that offered a free evening meal. Each day was a matter of survival on the most basic level, which taught Ellie to be grateful for the most basic and simple things. There was also the ongoing fear of being stopped by police, who were always on the lookout for runaways.

During this time, Ellie saw several people, including her close friends, fall victim to "downers." Ellie grew angry at the reckless behavior of people under the influence of drugs. She watched in horror as one friend fell from the second floor balcony of the Student Union while stoned.

More and more, drugs seemed stupid to Ellie. One evening, someone offered her a hallucinogen and she took it. Thankfully, the friend offered to walk her back to where she was staying. It was after dark and as they went to cross a busy intersection, Ellie looked at the traffic light and couldn't remember if she was supposed to cross with a red or green light. Confused, she stepped out into traffic and her friend snatched her back to safety. She realized the very real danger she was in. That was the last time Ellie took drugs. So many of the people she knew lived for drugs, and almost all they talked about was getting stoned. After her life in Milwaukee, Ellie could find pleasure just in being alive, in seeing a blue sky or hearing a bird sing. She thought it was sad that her friends couldn't face life without drugs or alcohol.

They spent hours and hours walking along Telegraph Avenue, their faces painted and cow bells hanging around their necks, wearing patched jeans and t-shirts, and storing their belongings in a backpack. The smell of incense drifted out of "Head Shops" along the way. They would shoplift shampoo or fruit or candy and they learned which restaurants would give them free food at closing time. They regularly went to a donut shop and a fish and chips place where they would get whatever crumbs were left at the end of the day. Another trick to get food was to walk by restaurants and grab food the patrons left on their plates, before the busboy cleared the table. They also learned that grocery stores threw away dairy and other items when they hit the expiration date, so Ellie and her friends would climb into the dumpsters after closing and grab as much food as they could.

One day Ellie noticed a girl who was new to the area. She was tall and striking, and seemed rather boisterous. She began flirting with a friend of Ellie's, and soon the girl and Ellie's friend were involved romantically. The girl was aggressive and Ellie was intimidated by her, but they got along well due to Ellie's submissive nature. However, one day they were in the bathroom at the Student Union, and the girl asked Ellie a question about her boyfriend. She didn't like Ellie's answer, and Ellie was startled by a sudden blow to her face .The girl then grabbed her by the hair and slammed her head against the tiles on the wall. Ellie started pleading with the girl to stop. She threw Ellie to the floor and kicked her in the face. A UCB student who was in the bathroom fled in fear, and Ellie, now dazed and in pain, struggled to get back up. Her attacker turned away for a moment and was saying something to Ellie, but Ellie used it as an opportunity to run as fast as she could from the bathroom to the other side of the Student Union. She collapsed crying onto a chair and some students, concerned for her, tried to comfort her. About ten minutes later, the girl found her and said, "Come outside with me. I'm not done talking to you." A security guard approached and told them to leave.

Ellie looked at the girl and cried out, "I won't go out there with you. You'll kill me!"

The girl looked shocked, realizing there were witnesses and she wouldn't get away with harming Ellie, so she left without resisting.

Ellie was cared for by the students until her friends came. They took her to an apartment where she was welcomed by the tenants, one of whom was a nurse. Ellie stayed there for about a week, very nervous any time she had to leave, for fear she would run into her attacker.

Ellie asked her friends if they knew anyone in the country she could stay with. This latest incident, along with the drug problems of her friends, made her realize it was time to leave Berkeley. An acquaintance knew some people in Half Moon Bay who agreed to let Ellie stay with them, so one afternoon they hitched a ride there. It was night when they arrived and Ellie was shown to a bedroom. "I've never had my own room before!" she exclaimed.

It was a rustic old house rented by three young people, two Stanford University students and the girlfriend of one of them. They had decided to get away from the rat race and live a simple life. The young woman had been a debutante, but became disillusioned with that lifestyle while in college.

In the morning, Ellie got to see where they were. It was an old neighborhood of small homes, and the one she lived in was only yards from the beach. Every day Ellie looked out the window and was amazed to see how many different colors the ocean could be. All day and night they heard the soothing sound of ocean waves. Every evening was a glorious sunset, and Ellie spent many daylight hours walking along the shore. She had never been exposed to nature or to country life like this before and fell deeply in love with the wonders of creation. She was a country girl; she felt it in her heart.

Her roommates didn't have a television or a radio. They did have a turntable and a collection of records. Ellie, for the first time, was exposed to classical music and was moved by the rich melodies. They also had albums by Neil Young, and Ellie fell madly into infatuation with him and his music. One of her roommates had a guitar and Ellie was allowed to play it, which rekindled her interest in playing. She spent many hours perfecting her strumming and different techniques that friends along the way had taught her. She also wrote a number of songs.

It was a time of refuge from the world and introspection on life, but Ellie felt loneliness deep in her gut. She was free from Gordon, and she was with friends, but there was no one special to her, no one she belonged to. Not having family to turn to in times of need and the profound depth of aloneness were hard to bear at times. In an effort to have something close to her, she adopted a puppy from people who had a ranch on Skyline Boulevard. He was a black lab mix and she named him Star. He was a sweet, obedient dog and she grew to love him very much.

Eventually, she was asked to move out because the original tenants wanted to have the place to themselves. Ellie had been trying unsuccessfully to get work, and through a friend she got a temporary job with Easter Seals, taping free knives on coffee cans. It was monotonous work and the hours seemed to drag on forever. The job was in San Mateo, and for a while Ellie lived at a youth hostel called Damien House. It was there that she met Neil, a boy from southern California who was traveling and had spent a few nights at Damien House. He played guitar and they jammed together. When he left, he asked Ellie if she would write him. They remained friends for years.

The job at Easter Seals ended early and Ellie was invited to move in with a girl from work. She tried to find work, but jobs were extremely scarce at that time. She knew that jobs were abundant on the east coast, so she decided to go back there. Her dream now was to work and save money to buy some land in the country, and maybe start a commune. She knew she wanted the peace and beauty of country life, and living and working in the city for a while was the price she had to pay for it.

She was able to find a girl to hitchhike across the country with her, but she couldn't take Star. Ellie had heard that Neil Young had a ranch on Skyline. The people she got Star from had partied with him and his girlfriend, Carrie. She knew exactly where it was and decided to leave Star with him. She and her roommate drove to the ranch. There was a long road downhill, and eventually they came to his home. They saw a small lake. Neil and Carrie were in a rowboat so Ellie quickly shoved Star out of the car and her friend raced back up the hill. Star chased the car, yelping. Ellie sobbed and told her friend to stop. "We can't! You can't keep him!" her friend yelled back.

Ellie's heart broke to see Star trying to catch her. She knew he would be scared, but she hoped he would be loved and cared for by her favorite musician.

A few days later, Ellie was driven to San Francisco by her friend David, where she met the girl she would travel with for another part of her journey. David dropped them off at the freeway. The two girls stuck out their thumbs and were on their way.

Chapter Seventeen
Pennsylvania

Once again, Ellie had the chance to see many new places. They slept on the beach, under bridges, and in open fields. One night they stopped and laid their sleeping bags out in a field and fell asleep under the stars. When she woke the next morning, Ellie was startled to see a large cow staring at her from about three feet away! One of her friends said, "Don't say 'hamburger,'" and the group burst into laughter as they ran from the field.

When they got to Utah, the two girls were picked up by a Mormon man and his children. He took them home with him. They were fed and allowed to shower and sleep in his back yard. The next day, his wife drove them in to Salt Lake City where they hitched a ride to a small town.

Ellie and her friend had two boys hitching with them now. As they had in the south, they experienced hostility here. A pick-up truck drove by and its passengers yelled that if Ellie's group wasn't gone soon, they would come back and beat them up. Ellie was scared. No one was stopping to give them a ride.

Finally, they all decided to pool their money and bought an old car from a dealer across the street. It was a beat up old car they paid $100 for, but they were happy to be safe and free of the burden of hitching. They headed to Denver and the car struggled to make it over the Rockies. After numerous bouts of overheating, they arrived at a park in central Denver where they camped out for a few days and met a young man from Pennsylvania. He and Ellie spent a lot of time together, and he asked her to go back to Pittsburgh with him. He assured her that she could get a job there, so she went. It was a relief to have his van to take them all the way.

When they got to Pittsburgh, Michael took Ellie to see a friend of his who needed a roommate. Within a week, she had a new job at a hospital and a place to live with his friend, Patty. Some things changed and some remained the same. Her friends were now all college students, most of whom still lived at home, so they were much more stable than her previous friends. Still, the drug and alcohol problem continued. Every weekend Patty and their mutual friends did exactly the same thing. Everyone showed up at their apartment with several cases of beer, and they blasted music and partied loudly. They tried so hard to get Ellie to like beer, but she hated the taste. "It tastes like feet!" she said and wondered why they couldn't have a good time without it. They often kept her awake until the wee hours when she had to get up at six o'clock in the morning for work.

Ellie enjoyed her job at the hospital, and thought once again about becoming a nurse. Before she left Milwaukee, she had been accepted into a nursing program, but gave that up when she fled. The hospital she worked for had a school of nursing, and Ellie decided to apply. She took her SATs and got accepted for the class beginning in September 1972. Meanwhile, she often worked the evening shift at her job. Sometimes a friend could pick her up or a co-worker could drive her home, but often she had to take the bus and then walk about a mile to her home. Part of the way was on a well-lit main road, but the last three blocks were in a very dark residential area.

One night as Ellie was walking home, she noticed a man standing in a driveway across the street. She turned to go down her street and walked in the middle of the street to feel safer. Suddenly, Ellie was aware that the man was running down the street beside her. She began to run as fast as she could and screamed at the top of her lungs. Thankfully, she was only a few feet from her home. She ran up the steps and slammed the door shut. The man ran up behind her and slammed against the door. By now, her friends came racing down the stairs and neighbors had come out on their porches to see what was happening. Her friends ran out and tried to find him, but were unsuccessful.

The next day, Ellie pleaded with the head nurse to keep her off that shift, but other aides complained that it would be unfair. Every evening was tense for her after that. If she couldn't get a ride, she paid to take a cab home, but the drivers often made her uncomfortable, too.

During the time she lived in Pittsburgh, Ellie was able to get in touch with Kevin Flannery. He called her occasionally and wanted her to visit him in Milwaukee. As much as she wanted to see him, she was afraid to go back there. She also corresponded with Neil in Los Angeles, but she still felt lonely. She had boyfriends, but nothing lasted long-term and she felt a nagging desire to belong to someone. Overall, though, this was by far the best her life had been since leaving Wisconsin. She was able to enjoy her freedom more. Simple things, like being able to eat as much as she wanted of a favorite food, meant a lot to her. She also had stability for the first time. She was able to make plans and set goals instead of just living to survive.

In September 1972, Ellie packed her things and moved into the dormitory of the nursing school. She loved what she was learning and was able to form bonds with a circle of friends. Now she had people she could count on and felt less lonely. Still, every weekend and holidays she watched all the students head home to be with their families and return with bags of food and clothes that their parents had bought them while Ellie struggled to get by, working any odd job she could.

In her second year, she was offered a job on weekends working the switchboard for the school. They had a portable television set and she watched *All in the Family* and *Mary Tyler Moore* every Saturday evening while she worked. She also took on babysitting jobs, but was always reminded of what she was missing-a loving family.

It was fun to have a group of friends to hang out with all the time. The girls often got invitations to frat parties and there was almost always something to do. Eileen, one of the girls in her class, told her parents that Ellie didn't have a family and spent holidays alone at school. Her parents insisted that Ellie come and stay with their family. Ellie resisted at first, but finally gave in. This family would become her own family for the next three years. They took her in as one of their own and she spent most of her breaks there. They showed extraordinary kindness to her. They lived in Central Pennsylvania, in Amish country. Ellie thought Central Pennsylvania was beautiful and she loved being exposed to other cultures.

In her last year at nursing school, Ellie was feeling stressed by the pressures of school. She started experiencing tingling in her legs and dizziness. She was tested for multiple sclerosis and the results were inconclusive, but it was the beginning of evidence of how her body, in particular her nervous system, had been damaged by all the stress and fear she had experienced with Gordon. She seemed prone to illness, and the doctor assigned to the nursing school was often rude and insulting to her.

At one point, Ellie needed her appendix removed. About a week later, she began having severe pain in her abdomen and ran a high fever. The doctor mocked and dismissed her, and no one helped until one evening when her incision broke open in several places with large amounts of pus. The doctors sheepishly cauterized the area and she was left with a huge, ugly scar.

Ellie looked forward to graduation. She was almost 23 and was tired of having the school staff treat her like a child. She still longed to live in Colorado, but finally settled on Los Angeles. Neil lived there, and he had rekindled Ellie's interest in the Bible, so Ellie went to where she had friends that welcomed her. She worked for about six months at UCLA Medical Center in pediatrics, but found the intense stress of the job hard to cope with. She continued to lag behind in maturity and social skills, which tended to leave her feeling like an outcast. She once again longed for a calmer life.

A year later, she moved to the San Francisco area where she made some close friendships. She worked part-time in a nursing home and spent time working more intensely on her personal growth. In time, she married and would finally achieve her dream of motherhood. She had the security of a family of her own and a stable lifestyle.

At last, she had really broken free. Free to have a life of her own. Free from Gordon.

Chapter Eighteen
The Courage to Go On

You have just read the story of my life. My real name isn't Ellie, that was my mother's name. It was easier for me emotionally to write this in the third person. However, the experience has still been emotionally draining. I had always remembered these events and thought I was fine because I could talk about it freely. Then someone pointed out to me how detached I am when I relate my childhood. "Like it's happening to someone else," she said.

Writing this book was tough because, in order to really describe what happened to me, I had to relive it in my mind and FEEL what happened. I had nights when I woke with anxiety and had to assure myself that Gordon can't hurt me. I've had a depressed, uneasy feeling hanging over me, and a desire to rush through it and get it over with. It has also been hard to see reactions of people who love me as they read some of the book. My daughter read Chapter Two relating the death of my parents and began to cry. She was unable to continue as were others.

One positive way writing this has affected me is that it has given me more compassion for myself. Now that I am 52 years old with grown children, I can look at what happened to me through a parent's eyes. Writing it out chronologically made me appreciate just how much my siblings and I went through. I would like to take some time now to discuss how my childhood impacted my adult life. While many things are negative, ultimately, I have much encouragement to give to others who have gone through or are going through traumatic events of their own.

Past Relationships

First, I'd like to tie up some loose ends. I didn't see my sister for seven years after I left Milwaukee. During that time I had no idea where she was or what she might be going through. I was plagued by guilt that I had left her there with *him*.

When my first child was born, I felt sad that I didn't have any family to share it with. When she was three months old, I decided to take a leap of faith and contact Uncle Ed, my mother's brother. I hadn't seen him in many years. He was listed in the phone book, so I called. The first thing I did was make him promise that he wouldn't let Gordon know where I was. He swore that he wouldn't and was so happy to hear from me. I hadn't been allowed contact with him since I was nine years old, and I was now 25. He generously sent me many things he had saved from my mother-photographs, scrapbooks, her wedding rings, a mink jacket, silverware, her wedding veil. I told him I desperately wanted to find my sister, who by this time was 21.

Uncle Ed called Sally and asked for my sister's address. It turned out that she lived only about an hour away from me in San Raphael! I sent her a telegram, asking her to call me. She called the next day, but was distant and unfriendly at first. Gordon had poisoned her with lies about me, but as we talked she warmed up and realized I wasn't a crazed drug addict. She came to see us and met her new niece, who was now five months old. She spent the weekend with us almost every week, and we spent time trying to remember everyone from our childhood and reconnecting with people.

It turned out that Uncle Ed went to the same church as Sandy. He gave us her phone number and I called to thank her for taking such good care of us and told her what happened after she left. She was very tense and not pleased that I had called her. She said that after she left, Gordon had showed up at her mother's house with a gun, threatening to shoot himself if she didn't come back. I guess his affair with Doris wasn't enough for him. It was obvious that she wanted to forget this part of her past, and she seemed fearful that somehow this would bring Gordon back into her life. Aside from Sandy, most people seemed happy to hear from us. We got in touch with our brother, who we barely knew. Some relatives told us they had sensed something had been wrong when we lived with Gordon, but they didn't want to interfere. The philosophy of everyone there was to "mind their own business and not get involved."

Although my sister had left Milwaukee to get away from Gordon, thankfully he had not abused her or controlled her as badly as he did with me. She was even allowed to have a job and a car while in high school, and to hang out with friends. Still, Gordon was Gordon, and she wanted to get away. Gordon and Doris had bought a house together and put it in their son's name. After I left, all of Gordon's sons ended up finding out about Doris and hanging out there.

I wrote Sally a letter, but she didn't respond. I was happy to learn that a few years after I left, Sally had gotten better. She lost weight and even started a home business. She was also busy helping her sons with their children. I was happy to know her life had gotten better. Still, I would have loved to have had her as a real mother to me.

One of the saddest things in my adult life is not getting to see my children through my parents' eyes. They didn't have grandparents because my husband's parents had also died when he was a teenager. I deeply missed not being able to share my pregnancies and births with my mother and enjoy her help and guidance in parenting. My children never got to know my parents and missed out on so much family history. Seeing the help my friends got from their mothers when a new baby came along and seeing the joy those grandmothers had always made me feel sad and a little bitter.

I wish I could have at least had a relationship with Sally. I think she would have been a good grandmother. I had to give that up in order to be free of Gordon. I probably had more fear than I needed to have, but I honestly didn't relax until I was about 40, because by then I knew he was too old to harm me or my family. After I tried unsuccessfully to rekindle a relationship with Sally, I gave up and didn't contact her again until a few years ago, when I wrote to her and sent pictures of my family. I never heard back from her. It makes me sad that now she's too old for me to have any closure with her or to restore contact. I lost my chance, if it was ever there.

Gordon got away with what he did to me. That is hard for me to live with. I like to think I got the best vengeance by breaking free from him and living a happy life. My sister told me that there were times when he seemed restless and nervous, and Doris told her that it was because he had heard I was back in town. Was he afraid? Did he worry that I would get him in trouble, or that my friends would harm him? That would certainly be a measure of justice, if he lived a tormented life after I left.

And of course, he lost control over me and the hope of whatever life he had planned to have with me. Still, it doesn't seem enough. He should have spent the rest of his life behind bars. I can't help but wonder how many girl hitchhikers he picked up and assaulted, or if he ever molested his granddaughters. He has children by at least three different women, all of the relationships overlapping. I found out he also has a daughter around my age (which may mean a fourth woman he impregnated), and it wouldn't surprise me if there are more of his progeny out there.

One of my aunts saw him at a funeral years ago and said he had bypass surgery and looked awful. If he spent the past 20 years suffering in poor health after all his chain smoking and drinking, it would be well deserved.

Would I have liked to tell him off? I have thought about it a few times, but never went through with it, for two reasons. One is that I very much doubt he would ever take any accountability. The other is, it wouldn't be worth the emotional upheaval I would suffer in seeing him again. Once I left, I never called to speak to him or Sally.

One question that always comes up with victims of abuse is, *Have you forgiven him*? It's thought to be healthy to forgive and let go of the past. I believe that forgiveness in its truest form must be preceded by remorse. What my uncle did to me was unforgivable if not regretted. He not only never showed remorse, but when he became aware of how profoundly his conduct affected me, he continued to do it. I have no basis to forgive him, since he did nothing to make things right. That being said, I have let go of the effect his actions had on me. I don't dwell on what happened or have anger over it. It is something I chose to forget, as much as possible. I don't think that I hate him, but I have no feelings of compassion toward him as I do with my aunt. I prefer for him to be a non-entity in my life.

Questions

You may have wondered as you read this why I didn't consider running away rather than suicide. The answer is that I had nowhere to go. I didn't have any money, and because I had not been allowed to work or have friends outside of school, I had no means or options for escape. There was also a realistic fear that I would be caught and my life would be a thousand times worse. It was hard for me to feel hopeful of being rescued. Even when there had been a glimmer of hope in that regard, Gordon managed to prevent it. I had thought of going to Uncle Ed, but Gordon would have gotten me back. In those days, there wasn't the awareness or sensitivity towards abuse, and people preferred to look the other way. I was so terrified, despondent, and without hope that death seemed the only sure escape. I have never again in my life, no matter what I went through, looked to suicide as an option. In my teens, it was truly an act of pure desperation.

I have been asked about the cause of my parents' death. My mom died of a massive brain hemorrhage, most likely an aneurysm. Uncle Ed told me that my mom had taken a bad fall down some stairs as a child, and they wondered if that was the cause. She had been complaining of headaches for a while before her death, but they had been attributed to stress.

My dad had a heart attack before my mom died, while he was still in his late 20s or early 30s. Heart disease claimed all his brothers at a young age.

My daughter asked me an interesting question. "Do you think your dad killed himself?" I don't know. The way he looked at me that day while I was brushing my teeth was definitely as if he *knew* he was going to die, that he wasn't going to see me again. He didn't seem upset. He was very calm; in fact, he seemed relieved, at peace.

An uncle said my dad had told him shortly before that, "If I'm not around, make sure the kids have gifts for Christmas." Now whether my dad knowingly did something with his medication or if he had been having cardiac symptoms that led him to believe he would die soon, I don't know. All I was told was that he showed up at the hospital and while waiting in line to check in, he collapsed. The doctors said he had a massive heart attack, and though he lived for a few hours, he never regained consciousness.

There was something in me as a little girl that wanted to save my dad from the unhappiness he felt after my mom's death. It is something that plagues me to this day. If I see someone sitting alone, my heart breaks for them. It also is sad to me that we weren't enough for him. As a parent, I wonder how my dad could have looked at me so calmly that day, knowing he was leaving me alone. Why didn't he arrange for someone to take us in? I guess he assumed his family would step up and care for us. He was so wrong, but I have to believe he never imagined the tortured lives we would have.

I don't feel anger towards my dad, but I do feel he abandoned us. I think he was lost without my mom and didn't know how to carry on. The humiliation of what happened with Maria was the last straw. I feel bad for my half sister because she never knew my father, and has never had a relationship with my siblings and I.

Parenting

I have to be very grateful to my mom because her loving, nurturing example is what I naturally patterned my own parenting after. I'm deeply grateful for having my first seven years with her. I was concerned that once my children got older, and especially in their teens, I would turn into Sally. That didn't happen, though, and I maintained a good relationship with all of my children throughout their teen years.

My biggest problem was that I had a morbid fear of leaving them with anyone. I couldn't get past the fear that anyone besides me would mistreat them, or at least, not be as caring. I can count on one hand the times my children were left with a sitter. I never worked outside the home because I wanted to always be available for them. I wanted them to have lots of memories of me in case I should die. I had a fear of that also-that I would die like my mom had.

I also have fears any time my children leave me. My 15-year old son said to me recently, as I was panicking over an outing he had planned with friends, "Mom, the worst thing isn't always going to happen." My poor kids have spent years hearing the worst case scenario from me. What they don't understand is that my own childhood was filled with things that most people never imagine happening. Worst case scenarios are what I came to expect and it has been hard, even after decades, to let go of that fear.

I also took an opposite approach from Sally and went too far in the other direction. I didn't make my kids do chores and was very easy on them. I always made sure they liked their clothes and avoided embarrassing them. In retrospect, I wish I had been a bit more structured with them but on the positive side, they are all loving, polite, caring people. My greatest pleasure was to stand in the doorway of the living room, observing my kids without them knowing. I saw kids who were confident, happy, and secure. They enjoyed their life in a carefree manner. That meant more to me than anything. For any deficiencies and mistakes I made along the way, I think the gift of those qualities is invaluable. That is a state of mind I never enjoyed past the age of 11.

Health Issues

As an adult, I have never had great health or stamina. Maybe it was a hereditary predisposition, but I also believe that my growing body was damaged by living under constant stress. Several things happened in my late 20s. After years of traveling and changes that I easily adapted to, all of a sudden I began having panic attacks. It began one day when I was speaking in front of friends and suddenly felt very dizzy and nauseous. A few weeks later, it happened at the mall and I felt the need to flee. Soon, I was having trouble any time I felt hemmed in by a crowd without a quick escape option, like an exit or bathroom. It would be years before I found out what it was- agoraphobia.

For me, it's the fear of being trapped. Even though I realize that it originates from my entrapment with Gordon, I can't control it. Knowing I am being unreasonable doesn't stop the physical reaction I get. As a result, I haven't been able to drive on the freeway in years. I don't go to movies or sporting events. I time errands like shopping so that I avoid crowds. Going to an appointment with a doctor or other office setting is also challenging for me. I have found ways to cope so that I still get things done and get out of the house, but I really am a prisoner to this as there are so many things I cannot do.

When I was 28, another change happened. This was one year after I began having panic attacks. I awoke in the middle of the night to what sounded like someone breaking into our apartment. That was one of my biggest fears and an intense panic came over me. I rushed into the living room but found that no one was trying to get in. I went back to bed with my heart pounding in my chest. I tried to go back to sleep, but my heart kept racing. I began sweating and feeling short of breath, as well as anxious. After trying to calm down for about an hour, I woke my husband and we went to the emergency room. They brushed it off as a good scare, but I was convinced that I had serious heart problems. After all, I saw family members drop like flies from heart disease throughout my childhood.

Over the next week, we went to the ER every night with the same problem. I would have spontaneous episodes of racing heartbeat and felt anxious all the time. I was finally admitted to the hospital, where I was diagnosed with mitral valve prolapse, a benign heart problem, and put on a beta blocker. It took several months before I felt back to normal. It was four years later that I had another flare-up (and it lasted for several months), and another seven years after that.

In 1994, my husband and I split up. I was left with traumatized kids, financial problems, and a lot of adjustments to make. We had become foster parents several years before, and with my nursing background I was qualified to care for infants with serious medical problems. I continued to do that as it was work I really believed in, and I knew I couldn't handle the high stress environment of working as a nurse. Also, I wanted to be available for my kids, which has proved to be a blessing long-term for them.

I was running myself ragged with my own children as well as foster babies who had many doctor appointments and hospital stays. I had one foster child who was placed with me as a newborn. He had been very premature, and as a result, had severe cerebral palsy, a colostomy, and for a while, a tracheotomy. I cared for him until he was six years old. As he grew, the demands of lifting him and getting him into various braces and equipment, as well as dealing with surgeries and therapies was a heavy burden.

Late in 2000, I had a quick succession of scary and upsetting events happen, including some frightening car problems, a bad fall, and financial setbacks. One night in January 2001, I awoke to my heart racing and a feeling of panic. I tried to calm myself down and over the next few days and weeks tried to reassure myself that it would pass. I had been through it before. However, it got worse, rather than better.

The doctor tried several SSRI anti-depressants to control the anxiety, but I had very bad reactions to them, which made my symptoms even worse. I was miserable all the time. I felt like I wanted to jump out of my skin. Often I would pace for hours trying to cope with the anxiety. Sounds, like someone opening a door, would reverberate through my head. I had constant tingling in my arms and legs, and ringing in my ears. I had insomnia even though I felt extremely tired. I had days when I was very anxious, and then I would have what I called "crash days" because I felt very tired and depressed.

It would be some time before I knew what was wrong with me. It was adrenal exhaustion, which was caused by prolonged stress. My body just gave out. I suffered for six months before getting some relief with hormone replacement therapy and a different beta blocker. That was the summer of 2001, and I still live with chronic fatigue. My nervous system still reacts badly if I overdo it or am under stress.

One of the worst things for me is to run a fever. It takes weeks to recover. I take handfuls of supplements daily, which I have spent a small fortune on with only slight improvement in my health. I think my body has been through too much stress in my lifetime, and is now saying "no more." I am careful now to keep my life as simple as possible, and stress to a minimum.

Social Inadequacies

It is discouraging to cope with these problems. I have been handicapped emotionally and socially because of my childhood, and now I have physical limitations as well. It has been heartbreaking to me many times over the years to see how badly I have been affected by the past.

Although, overall, I function very well, close friendships have been a challenge. Deep insecurity and lack of confidence and self-esteem have caused me at times to be clingy, jealous, and too dependent on people I get close to. I am still the little girl looking for someone to nurture and love her. Facing the reality that no one is going to do that is very painful.

In my 20s, my social skills were atrocious at times. I have always been immature socially for my age. In my teens and twenties, I tended to be much too blunt in what I said and offended people. In an effort to avoid those reactions, I swung the other way and became a people pleaser.

It took many years of watching others whom I admired to slowly develop the kind of personality I wanted. Only in the past five years or so have I been able to conduct myself with graciousness, kindness, and a more lighthearted spirit.

Criticism is hard for me to take, but thankfully, I have always been introspective and able to see and then change things that people have brought to my attention. It is hard after my childhood not to be cynical. I have to work hard at not being a negative person.

The Worst Part about Child Abuse Is We Are Victimized Twice

There is the initial abuse we endure as children, and then the difficulties with relationships and even social isolation we experience as adults. It is an ongoing game of catch up. There are also the unfulfilled dreams and potential. If I hadn't been plagued with agoraphobia, I probably could have pursued more of my childhood dreams as an adult.

Children survive abuse because they have no choice. It doesn't usually involve courage or inner strength; we were trapped in a situation we couldn't escape. The courage comes later, when we are old enough to be free. It takes courage and strength to grow beyond the dysfunction that is all we know.

I see so many parents of my foster babies who are still trapped in their adolescence, even though they may be in their 30s or 40s. I want to encourage everyone that you can break free of the lifestyle you may feel trapped in. Alcohol and drug dependence, crime, gangs, and similar things won't bring you peace or true happiness in your life. It won't bring you or your family security or hope. The courage comes now, as you reach for something better for yourself and for your children.

Final Words of Inspiration

In spite of everything, I try to look at my life each day with gratitude. If I am feeling down, all I have to do is mentally put myself back in Milwaukee and I know that no matter what happens to me now, nothing can be that bad. It makes me appreciate every good thing in my life. Sometimes I have to remind myself of that when I feel negative or worried (and I am a worrier!).

I have a lot to be thankful for. I got to be a mom, which was my heart's desire. I have friends whom I love. I have seen my sister really take charge of her life and be very successful. My brother, after years of being single due to fear of abandonment, married my sister-in-law and I now have two beautiful nieces.

I have faith in God and reliance on the Bible that has guided me to be the best I can be. And while I am aware of my shortcomings, I'm very happy that I was able to keep a loving heart, a generous and caring spirit, and a desire to do good.

I Made a Conscious Decision to Use My Life for Good

When I was still in my late teens, I knew I didn't want to repeat the behavior that I was raised with. I knew that I wanted to rise above it and be a better person. It would be convenient to use my childhood as an excuse to be cruel or unproductive, but that would only harm others and myself. I gain far more happiness by taking a better road.

I have given back and sort of cancelled out my childhood in a sense. By being a foster parent for over 15 years and caring for over 45 children so far, I have been able to do for them what I wish someone had done for me.

This has been the story of my life. Writing it has been harrowing for me. I am tired of this being my life story; I want to trade it in for another. Now that I am 52, it pains me to know that this is what I am stuck with. At the same time it has made me strong, compassionate, and grateful.

I wish I could have had a large, close, extended family. I wish my children had grandparents and lots of cousins. I wish I didn't have an empty hole in my heart that never closes. But we take what we have and do the best we can with it. My best piece of advice is this:

Even if no one else loves you, love yourself.
Give yourself the love and life that you deserve.

Poems

Thankful

Before the pain,
I never saw the sun rise
before my heart ached,
I never felt the breeze on my face
before I cowered in fear,
I never knew the joy of being alive
before I was free,
I never knew the joy of being me
before I was put through the fire,
I never heard the birds sing

I reached out my hand in the darkness
searching for another to hold
searching for arms to keep me safe
there were none
and so I learned to be strong
I learned to have faith
I learned to endure

And now I rejoice with each day
with each simple thing
nothing is taken for granted

what a gift it was
to have so much pain
to get in the end
this gift of joy
to be so
thankful.

Abandonment

This hole is so deep
the wound endlessly unhealed
why can't I ever shut this door?
Why does it always come back to haunt me?

You left me so vulnerable and alone
I know you didn't mean to
One of you had no choice
the other could have tried harder
Your own pain overshadowed concern
You trusted they would care for us
they didn't

A lifetime of loving and hoping hasn't erased
the empty hollowness you left
No one has been able to fill that hole
The need is a millstone around my neck
No matter how hard I try
I can't appease it

Sometimes I tire of this fight
to be ok when I can't be ok
To be fulfilled while I have this huge hole
that you left behind
Where do I go?

Sometimes I feel strong
some days I feel released
but the empty hole is always there
waiting to be filled.

Printed in the United States
58365LVS00006B/201